HY-11

W9-AFG-481

AUG   2008

The
Hell
Merchant

**Center Point
Large Print**

**This Large Print Book carries the
Seal of Approval of N.A.V.H.**

The
Hell
Merchant

Ray Hogan

CENTER POINT PUBLISHING
THORNDIKE, MAINE

This Center Point Large Print edition
is published in the year 2008 by arrangement with
Golden West Literary Agency.

Copyright © 1972 by Ray Hogan.
Copyright © renewed 2000 by Gwynn Hogan Henline.

The text of this Large Print edition is unabridged. In other
aspects, this book may vary from the original edition.
Printed in the United States of America.
Set in 16-point Times New Roman type.

ISBN: 978-1-60285-239-6

Library of Congress Cataloging-in-Publication Data

Hogan, Ray, 1908-
    The hell merchant / Ray Hogan.--Center Point large print ed.
      p. cm.
    ISBN: 978-1-60285-239-6 (lib. bdg. : alk. paper)
    1. Large type books. I. Title.

  PS3558.O3473H38 2008
  813'.54--dc22

2008009487

1 ~~~

It was a land of majestic beauty, of stirring grandeur, Starbuck thought, easing forward on his saddle as the sorrel loped tirelessly on.

To the west the mighty Sangre de Cristo Mountains, like a towering wall dividing the universe, lifted into a hazy, afternoon sky. Pine, fir, golden-clad aspen and triangular-shaped spruce studded slopes peppered with nodding blue asters, and in the higher levels snow already banked the layered ledges and rugged peaks with glistening white. Here and there a worn face of granite bared its storm-swept surface to the winds as it lay steeped in the secrets of the past, content with memories while it defied time and man.

He'd heard wolves challenging the stars that previous night when he camped, and in the early morning as he moved out, he had twice seen herds of deer, the does with their huge ears cocked forward, the bucks sporting rocking chair racks of antlers as they bounded through the piñon and cedar groves on the lower flats.

Settling back he looked over his shoulder. Behind him lay the rolling hill and grass land that stretched on to the east—to Kansas and farther. Bathed now in the amber glow of the lowering sun, it appeared soft, gentle—and brought to his mind the realization that night was near, that he should be looking for a suitable campsite. He was yet three days out of Santa Fe and had expected to be closer to the mountains by that sundown, but it was evident that he would fall short. He shrugged; it had happened before, this misjudging of distance in the startlingly clear atmosphere.

He disliked camping on open ground and so swung his attention ahead to a not too-distant mass of rock and timber thrusting upward from the surrounding land. That would be Cold Water Mountain, he supposed. There would be a creek and places that enabled him to escape the early morning wind that always came just before sunrise. He'd ride on, make his night stop there.

Touching the gelding with spurs, Starbuck moved on, the sharp, crisp promise of winter in the air definite in his nostrils. It wouldn't be long until icy storms would roar in from the lofty peaks of the Colorados to the north, and the vast country would fall silent under a numbing blanket of white, become a danger to all those who did not respect or know its subtle ways.

The old Santa Fe Trail was behind him, the cutoff favored by some, on farther east. He had crossed the main route earlier, had been surprised to find no one pursuing its deeply rutted course. But it was October—late—and he guessed it was only normal. His own plans called for getting out of the high country before winter set in; he'd go on to Arizona immediately if he failed to find Ben in Santa Fe.

Ben . . . Shawn Starbuck's square-cut features grew thoughtful. A tall, lean man, not long out of boyhood, he sat in his saddle in an easy, offhand manner. His eyes, gray-blue in the slimming light, were overhung by a shelf of thick brows and the dark hair, inclined to curl about his neck when he neglected to trim it, as it was now, had a deep, glossy sheen.

He appeared much older than his years. The change that had come upon him when he was turned from an Ohio farm boy into a trail rider in quest of a brother had quickly weathered him, laid its mark upon him to the point where age was indeterminate and there was no calculation in time. Trouble, danger, bitter disappointment and experience had interfused to turn boy into man, convert youth to age without the building of days.

But if he were aware of the rapid transition, Shawn did not regret it, and the life of constant motion he led never palled, perhaps because it had all begun in his early years and he knew no other.

There was no denying, however, there were times when he felt a tug at his heart and the pointed pangs of loneliness did catch up and fill him with a dark thoughtfulness. He would dwell then upon what might have been, on a life purely his own with no hampering strings attached; he would remember his dream of a home, a ranch, a woman such as Rhoda Hagerman whom he'd met in faraway south Texas, or the quiet-faced girl in Hebren Valley.

They, and others, had much to offer and he'd felt the stirring need to halt, to settle down, take a wife and fulfill his own needs, but in the end he had faced up to the duty that, like an unbending bar of steel, dictated his way of life. All such must be denied him until he found

Ben and the matter of Hiram Starbuck's estate was settled. . . . But—someday—

Shawn brushed his hat to the back of his head, stared at the gradually approaching mountain where he intended to make camp. Day's-end hush had fallen over the land and the purple heads of the bunch grass that carpeted the flats and slopes were nodding slowly from side to side in the faint breeze. . . . It would be good to stop, to climb down from the sorrel's back; he'd been in the saddle since sunup and the muscles of his legs were beginning to take note of the fact.

Somewhere off to the right a quail called into the quiet—the sound plaintive and lost. The small, blue-scaled birds would have their nesting done by now and be gathering into coveys. A brace would make a tasty evening meal if he had some means of getting them. Back on the farm he and Ben had often trapped them, brought them in to their mother, Clare, as a special table treat. . . . But that was another day, another time —another world.

He shrugged off his thoughts. He was in no mood to remember, to think of how it had been once. His mind now wanted only to consider the present; bed down for the night, then on to Santa Fe with the sun. If Ben wasn't there, move on. Ben could be anywhere in that broad expanse known as the frontier.

It was a task best taken as it came. *All journeys begin with the first step,* he had heard his schoolteacher mother say many times. *Each thing done must have a beginning.* So it was with him, so it had been—and so

8

it would be until, at last, he found Ben and the quest would end.

He drew the sorrel to a slow walk, eyes now on the dark green of the mountain just ahead. A short distance within it he caught the faint sparkle of silver; a creek. That was where he would halt. Veering the gelding around a rocky, brush-cluttered mound, he angled for that point.

He pulled to a stop in a small coulee bordered on one side by the murmuring stream, the other by low bushes and by rocks that had in times past come tumbling down the steep slopes during the wild storms that periodically lashed the area.

The last of the sun's rays were fanning up in the west, filling the sky with a riotous blend of gold, yellow, and orange across which an arrowhead of geese knifed its way. He watched the migrating flock briefly and then turned aside, aware that he had little time left in which to prepare his camp before darkness set in. But that realization did not move him to undue haste.

He remained in the saddle while the sorrel stretched its neck and bobbed its head impatiently toward the stream, allowing its eyes to probe the brush and the deep shadows behind the rocks intently. He could neither hear nor see anything, man or beast, yet Shawn was conscious of an uneasiness.

The quail called again into the stillness, and far up on the mountain a coyote barked a reply. Starbuck's wide shoulders twitched, and swinging off the sorrel, he led it to the water. He waited a few moments, permitting the big horse only a few swallows, and then drew him away; he could take his fill later after the heat was gone from his body.

Shawn glanced again to the western sky, judged he'd best collect his firewood while there was still some light, tend the sorrel later. Picketing the animal, he began to rustle up dry limbs, branches, and other bits of litter that would burn, moving about slowly, quietly, the strong feeling that he was not alone, that he was being watched, yet plaguing his mind.

He piled what he considered a sufficient quantity of fuel in the center of the clearing and crossed back to the gelding. Tripping the tongue of the cinch buckle, he pulled off the hull, draped it over a log in a fashion designed to keep the stirrup flaps and skirt straight, and then spread the padded blanket over it to shed the night's moisture. That done, he carried his bedroll and saddlebags to the coulee and dropped them near a fair-sized rock and, squatting, began to assemble some of the wood for a fire.

Starbuck came up fast, hearing a quick step behind him. His left hand swept down instinctively for the low-slung pistol on his hip, dropped away as an iron hard fist crashed into the side of his head.

Dazed, he went over sideways, and again from instinct, rolled fast as a towering shape surged toward him through a thin, gray haze. He gained his feet, and slightly off balance, met the oncoming figure with a stiff left and a wide, swinging right.

The man grunted as the blows drove home, but he did not falter. Shawn fell back before the crowding hulk, the flailing arms. He took a sharp rap to the head, another to the ribs. He was having difficulty getting set, planting his feet squarely under him on the uneven ground. A skilled fighter, well trained by old Hiram, he could hold his own ordinarily in any sort of combat—catch as catch can, or scientific—but he had been taken off guard, and, dazed at the outset, his reflexes were dull and not functioning efficiently.

He sought to back away, allow his brain to clear, his legs to steady, but the powerful stranger was giving him no chance; he continued to bore in, hammering furiously, relentlessly with big, hamlike fists, and Shawn could find time only to ward off the sledging blows.

The mist was fading slowly from his eyes. He was beginning to shake off the effects of the initial onslaught. His breathing had evened and he felt strength coming back into his legs. . . . A few moments more and he would be in condition to reply to the attack in kind.

. . . *If you get in bad trouble,* Hiram had once told him, *back off, and keep backing 'til you get your head again. Then your chance will come.*

Starbuck, arms now raised in a rigid, protective stance, continued to move, to feint from side to side as he deflected the blows directed at him. . . . A big man, one with a thick, black beard, hard, glittering eyes, and broad, strong teeth. Anger flared through Shawn. What

11

the hell was this all about? Who was the stranger—and why did he jump him? As far as he could recall they'd never crossed trails before. The anger cooled as quickly as it had come, leveled off into grimness. Those were questions he'd get the answer to shortly.

Eyes narrowed, watchful, Shawn fell back a long step, dodged as the man lunged forward in his wake. He snapped a punishing left to the side of the dark face, followed with a right that cracked as it landed. An ordinary man would have dropped to his knees from the blow, but the bearded giant only grunted, paused, and then came on.

Shawn struck again quickly, staggered him with another hard swing, capped it off with a stinging left to the eyes, and took a step away, once more laying a trap.

His motion was checked abruptly as a spur caught against an exposed root or some other obstacle on the ground. He rocked forward, tried to save himself from going over backwards. The bearded, distorted face was suddenly before him. A solid ball of knuckles rushed toward him through the dim light, connected squarely with the point of his chin, and he was lost in a fog of blackness.

2 ～～～

Starbuck opened his eyes slowly. His head ached and pain throbbed in his legs and arms. Without moving he stared about. It was full dark. The bearded man was hunched by the fire in the center of the coulee methodically stirring a concoction of some sort in a sooted spider with the blade of a skinning knife. A tin of coffee simmered at the edge of the flames.

The pain seeping through him was being caused by bonds drawn too tightly about his ankles and wrists, he realized, and he shifted slightly to ease the pressure of the buckskin thongs. The change did not draw the attention of his captor and Shawn continued to study him. . . . A big man, as he had noted at the start of the fight, well over two hundred pounds and probably an inch or two more than six feet in height. Burly and powerfully built, he was wide across the chest and his hairy arms were thick and muscular like those of men who followed the trade of blacksmith.

He had washed his face and combed the heavy shock of black hair that capped his head as well as brushing out the wedge of beard that jutted from the lower part of his features. Shawn could not see his eyes but he recalled them from before—hard and flashing, matching exactly the brutal set of the mouth.

Starbuck frowned as questions again pushed into his mind. What did the fellow want with him? That it was no holdup was apparent; he wouldn't be lying there trussed up like a sacrificial goat if that was the case—and the bearded man would have long since taken his leave. The same applied if, afoot for some reason, he had wanted the sorrel.

Considering his thoughts, Shawn swore silently, cursing the vagaries that somehow seemed to conspire in throwing problems onto the trails he followed. At times it seemed to him that luck or fate, or whatever it was that guided men's destiny, was determined that he should never find Ben.

The odor of cooking food began to hang in the coulee. It smelled good, stirred the hunger within Shawn; he hadn't eaten since daybreak, but the anger and resentment within him pushed the need aside. He pulled himself to a sitting position.

"Like to know what the hell this is all about," he said in a taut voice.

The bearded man paused in his stirring, looked up through bushy brows. "I ain't needing none of your lip."

"You're getting it anyway."

The man by the fire rose slowly, knife blade dripping. His eyes squeezed down into slots in which the glow of the flames reflected dully, and for a moment he seemed about to step across the narrow space that separated him from Starbuck and strike with the blade he was holding. And then he shrugged as if having second thoughts.

"You're my prisoner, that's what it's all about."

"Know that," Shawn said dryly. "Why?"

"Catching outlaws—that's my business," the big man said, squatting again and reaching for a tin plate. "You want some grub? I ain't caring one way or another whether you do or not."

Shawn nodded, continued to study the man at the fire. "I'm no outlaw," he said after a time. "Whoever you think I am, you're mistaken. I never saw you before—don't even know you—"

"Name's Hillister. Luke Hillister."

"Still makes you a stranger, and I doubt if you ever heard of me either—Starbuck."

"Names don't mean nothing. Can be changed easy," Hillister said. Taking up a second plate he filled it with the stew he had thrown together, again straightened to his full height, and circling the fire, placed the plate at Shawn's side.

"Ain't trusting you with something to eat with. Have to use your fingers," he said, looking down at Starbuck. "Now, I'm aiming to untie your wrists. You make a move to jump me and I'll kill you. Understand? Don't make a damn whether I hand you over to the law dead or alive. That plain?"

"It's plain," Starbuck said, leaning forward so Hillister could get to the leather linking his wrists. It was also clear what the problem was; Hillister, evidently some kind of a lawman, took him to be a wanted outlaw and was planning to turn him over to the nearest sheriff or marshal.

His hands came free suddenly and he dropped his arms, easing the pain in his shoulders, but not trusting Hillister, he remained motionless, waited until the man had returned to the fire. Then, picking up his own plate, he began to eat.

It was good stew—meat-chunked potatoes, onions, and some sort of greens apparently gathered along the creek. Shawn only barely noticed, and after a few bites, paused.

"You a lawman?"

15

Hillister's large head came up. "Kind of a special one. I take hold where them others leave off."

Shawn considered that, finally devised its meaning. "Bounty hunter," he murmured.

"There's some who call me that."

"Seems it fits."

Hillister wiped at his mouth with the back of a hand. "Ain't just the way you're a-figuring. Law's not what it ought to be. Soft, too easy on killers and the like. And them badge-toters, they ain't anxious to go out after the real outlaws. Make it my job."

"Well, you're wrong where I'm concerned. Not an outlaw. Never was."

"Sure wearing that gun like one."

Shawn stared. "That why you jumped me? That what you're going by?"

Hillister spat. "Good a sign as any."

"You're loco," Starbuck said flatly.

The bearded bounty hunter paused in his eating, eyes narrowing again. "That there lip of your'n is going to get—"

"Happens my first name was taken from an Indian word," Starbuck continued. "Looking at it the way you do that makes me an Indian. . . . Same kind of fool reasoning."

Luke Hillister relaxed, lifted the tin plate to his thick lips, and drained it of the last bits of stew. Setting it aside, he reached for the coffee.

"What're you doing in this part of the country?" he asked, conversationally.

"Riding through. On my way to Santa Fe. . . . I'll ask you the same question."

"Hunting two brothers, that's what—"

"And you saw me instead—grabbed me."

Hillister seemed not to be listening. Placing the can of coffee on the ground, he reached into an inside pocket, produced a small card. For several moments he was lost in the contemplation of it, and then returning it to his brush jacket, he once again took up the tin.

"You wanting a swallow of coffee?" he asked, thrusting it at Shawn.

Starbuck accepted, downed a mouthful of the black, bitter liquid. "That's the way of it, wasn't it?" he pressed, handing back the can.

"Like I said, catching outlaws is my job."

"Well, you've made a hell of a mistake this time," Shawn snapped in disgust.

"Maybe, but I'm misdoubting that. Ain't never been wrong before, so I ain't worrying none now." Hillister began to toy with the skinning knife, turning it over and over between his thick fingers while he cupped the tin of coffee with his free hand. "What're you heading to Santa Fe for? You meeting some of your friends there?"

"Looking for my brother. Chance he'll be there."

"Meaning you ain't sure?"

Shawn nodded. Perhaps if he told Luke Hillister of his purpose he might convince the man that he was no outlaw.

"Just don't know. He ran off from home—Ohio—ten years ago. Been trying to find him, settle some family business. Name's Ben—or he could be calling himself Damon Friend."

The bounty hunter's eyes sharpened. "The law after him, too?"

Starbuck hesitated. There was a charge against Ben pending in southern New Mexico Territory. Nothing serious, the sheriff had assured him, but a matter that required his brother's presence to clear it up. He doubted Hillister would understand that, however; best he skirt the truth.

"Not an outlaw, if that's what you're driving at."

"Then why's he running and hiding?"

"Don't know that he is. Thing is we lost track of each other—and this is a big country to find a man in."

"Ain't so hard if a man's of a real mind. Been riding it plenty and I always find who I'm looking for. What's your brother look like?"

"Not sure. Expect we sort of look alike."

Hillister tipped the coffee can to his mouth, emptied it, dropped it to the ground. Far up on the mountain a coyote yipped into the night. The bounty hunter listened to the discordant sound for a time, finally shook his head.

"You think I'm believing a yarn like that? You ain't sure of his name and you don't know what he looks like—and you're traipsing all over the country hunting him! Mighty farfetched, was you to ask me."

"No more farfetched than your grabbing every man you run across that looks like an outlaw to you," Shawn replied quietly.

"Him changing his name—"

"Did that after he had a ruckus with our pa. Said he didn't want any connection with the family. And how he looks—been ten years—we were just kids when I saw him last. Man changes plenty when he grows out of being a boy."

Hillister, lightly rubbing the swelling under his left eye where Shawn's fist had left its mark, grunted, shrugged his shoulders. Reaching into his jacket again, he produced the card he'd viewed earlier, once more fell to considering it. It could be a picture, a tintype, Starbuck decided. Evidently it meant much to the bounty hunter.

"Riding like you say you do, you ever run across a man you think might be him?"

Luke Hillister pocketed the picture, and leaning forward, began to collect the utensils scattered near the fire.

"Don't recollect nobody like that," he said without stopping. "Name sure ain't familiar. There's a bite or two of this sonofabitch left. You want it?"

Shawn glanced at the spider Hillister held out to him. The remainder of the stew, cold now, was little more than caked grease.

"Had enough," he said. "What're you aiming to do next?"

The bounty hunter came to his feet, the frying pan, plates, coffee tin, and spoons, together with his skinning knife, all clutched in his big hands.

"We're sleeping right here tonight," he replied.

"Then, comes tomorrow, I'm doing you a favor. I figure you're a goddamn, no-account outlaw—you're claiming you ain't—so I'm trotting you back to Cimarron and letting Bart Trueman—he's the sheriff—look you up. When he gets the wanted dodger out on you, you'll see I know what I'm doing."

"He won't find one," Starbuck said, and let it drop. The sheriff would settle it—but Cimarron was north, in the opposite direction of Santa Fe. It meant losing a day or more.

"You'll be wasting your time and mine," he said, sighing. "But if that's what it'll take to convince you, I'm for it. . . . Like it better if we headed south, however."

"No sheriff that way—not until we get clean to Santa Fe—and I ain't aiming to be bothered with you that long. Got other cats to skin."

"Those two brothers?"

Hillister bobbed his head, moved toward the creek with his collection of pans. "Live around here somewheres and Santa Fe's three days' riding. Cost me a whole week was I to take you there. Can get to Cimarron tomorrow."

"Still means you'll lose two days and those brothers could get away. Turning me loose now—"

"You ain't doing nothing but blowing your breath," the bounty hunter said without pausing. "We're camping here and going to Cimarron tomorrow. . . . Now, set quiet while I wash up these here things. You make a move to get away and I'll put a bullet in your

20

head. Easier to haul your kind in across a saddle, anyway. Less bother."

"Expect it is, only when you're wrong you've got murder on your hands."

"Ain't ever been wrong yet—and I don't figure I am with you."

"Comes a first time for everything," Starbuck said and lay back.

His hands were free and he could get to the knife he carried inside his left boot, slice through the buckskin binding his ankles. But it would be a mistake; Hillister was watching him closely, would shoot him down the instant he made a try to escape. Best to wait for a better opportunity—the bounty hunter could forget to tie his wrists or possibly get careless and, at close quarters, turn his back. Then would be the time to act.

3 ~~~

Luke Hillister did not forget. After completing his cleaning chore, he had crossed to where Shawn lay, roughly pulled the tall rider's arms behind his back, and tied them firmly at the wrists with the same strip of rawhide. In that position Starbuck spent an uncomfortable night. Although he tried for an hour or more after the bounty hunter had fallen asleep to work his fingers into the boot where he carried his knife, he found it impossible and eventually gave it up.

Silent, an early morning sourness claiming him, Hillister prepared a quick breakfast of fried meat, warmed bread, and coffee, and not long before sunrise they were mounted and striking north for Cimarron. The bounty hunter took no chances; he again restored the bonds to Starbuck's wrists, removed only those that linked his ankles, thus permitting him to bestride the sorrel. As an additional precaution, he attached a lead rope to the gelding's bit ring and fastened it to his own saddle in pack-horse fashion.

Shawn had given Hillister a great deal of thought during the long, cold night. That the man was no ordinary manhunter had become evident to him. With Hillister it was a passion bordering on a mania and unquestionably ranged far beyond the matter of cash reward. He appeared to be a man more on a crusade of vengeance, one driven by a determination to track down and kill or capture any and all malefactors regardless of situation or circumstances.

There was something chewing on the big, dark bearded man, Starbuck finally concluded, something out of the past that possessed him, turned him into a ruthless, single-minded killer at large.

"This business of yours," Shawn said after a lapse of several miles had occurred; "you work out of some town—some lawman's office?"

Hillister shook his head. "Ain't got no use for badge-toters. Done told you that."

"Then how do you collect your rewards?"

"Only time I ever have something to do with them."

"You called the sheriff at Cimarron by name. Guess you've done business with him before."

Hillister was looking up, his gaze following the graceful dipping and gliding of an eagle high above a line of palisades to their left.

"Been a couple of times," he replied. "But we ain't friends. Ain't never no friend of a lawman."

Starbuck shifted on his saddle. It would be pleasant riding through the broad, green country had it been under different conditions. The air was cool and fresh and the miles-distant peaks around them appeared to be within easy reach.

It brought to his mind the words an old Arizona prospector had uttered once when they were standing on the edge of a bluff and looking out over a vast panorama of country: *so clear a man could see all the way to the Pearly Gates,* had been his observation. So it was there in far northern New Mexico, but Shawn was getting little enjoyment from it.

The buckskin was cutting into his wrists and the forced position of his shoulders was causing the muscles of his back to throb. He thought again of the knife in his boot, estimated his chances of getting it. It would require leaning far over, working it out of its sheath with the tips of his fingers, and then, after reversing the bone-handled blade, manipulating it in a manner that would cut through the tough thongs.

It would be risky; Hillister glanced back periodically —and the process would require time. Like as not they would reach Cimarron long before he could complete the task. Best he just swallow his pride and indignation and hope the sheriff—Bart Trueman the bounty hunter had called him—would be in his office when they arrived and could clear things up to Hillister's satisfaction.

He settled his eyes on the bounty hunter's thick shoulders, moved his arms again to ease the dull pain. "You making much money doing this?"

Luke Hillister stirred. "Can't see as that's any of your business!"

"Maybe not. Was only wondering. Long as you've been at it, seems you ought to have a pile by now."

"Well, I ain't. Living—what I've got to pay for—takes most of it. Been saving some for the day when I—"

The big man's voice trailed off into silence. Shawn realized he had struck a chord deep within Hillister, one that could lead to an understanding of the darkness that filled him.

"Guess everybody's got something in mind he's working and hoping for."

"Reckon so. Ain't always easy to come by, however."

"Nothing good ever is."

"For a fact, but I'm getting it someday. Place of my own, place where I can take Ellie, make her happy and comfortable."

Luke's low voice faded into nothing again. Shawn said, "Ellie—she your wife?"

Hillister spat impatiently. "No need for you knowing that."

"Guess not, but if it's her you're working to get money for, this is one time you'll fail her."

Hillister muttered something, brushed at his face.

The day was beginning to warm as the horses plodded steadily on. Starbuck, twisting his arms, managed to loosen the buttons of his brush jacket and pull at the collar of his shirt, relieving the heat to some extent.

Another hour passed slowly by. They entered a long valley, crossed, climbed to the opposite rim. The horses were sweating freely and Hillister curved off the trail and halted in the shadow of a broadly spreading tree.

"Aiming to rest the animals a mite," he said. "Just you stay in the saddle."

Starbuck only shrugged. Dismounting, stretching his legs and moving about would have eased the cramp in his muscles, but he knew it would be useless to argue about it. Slumped forward, he watched the bounty hunter dig into his inner pocket again. Spurring the sorrel ahead carefully, he glanced over Hillister's shoulder. It was a tintype, one bearing the likeness of a woman and two young boys not yet in their teens. The woman was small and pretty.

"That your wife and sons?"

At the question Luke Hillister started violently. Jerking away, he thrust the photograph into his jacket and whirled. His broad face was angry and his dark eyes sparked.

"Keep your goddamn lip to yourself! I won't have the likes of you ever talking about them—hear?"

Shawn smiled. "Suit yourself. . . No sense in a man being touchy about his family, though. Fine looking, all of them."

"Shut up—ain't telling you again! Don't want you even a-thinking about them! You keep on and I'll take you on into Cimarron a-laying across your saddle. Now, get back—get back!"

Starbuck eased the gelding away. Hillister, his face glistening with sweat, eyes still bright, abruptly hauled up on the reins of his grazing horse, and, yanking at the lead rope, moved on.

Shawn urged the sorrel forward, breaking the sudden tautness of the line and permitting his mount to lower its head to the usual angle. He was convinced now that Luke Hillister was not quite sane. He had seen violence and death in the big man's eyes in those brief moments and he was glad now he had made no effort to escape. With the odds the way they were he most probably would have ended up, as the bounty hunter had threatened, across his saddle. He'd hold his peace until they reached Cimarron.

Strangely, it was Hillister who broke the silence several miles later. He had calmed and his voice was low and conversational, and he was evidently speaking thoughts that were running through his oddly twisted mind.

"This here working for something you want—a dream maybe some folks calls it—there ain't nothing wrong with a man doing that. . . . Sort of keeps him going when things get real tough. Ain't no reason why I can't have me a dream, same as other people."

Starbuck shook his head. "None at all."

"And getting it the way I do—sort of selling killers

and renegades into hell—there ain't nothing wrong with that either."

"Not when they have it coming to them."

"Just what I mean. Man earns what he gets. There's something in the Bible saying that a man living by the sword's going to be dying by it."

"Expect most outlaws know that's how it'll be for them. Part of the bargain they make with themselves."

"Getting caught and hung—that what you mean?"

"Sure. They know what's right and what's wrong, and they're willing to gamble on their chances of beating it out. Some do."

"And that's where I come in," Hillister said promptly. "I don't let them beat it. Just can't see why some folks look at me the way they do—like I was dead wrong—and treat me worse'n they do a dog because I'm doing it. . . . Not that I give a goddamn!"

"Probably because you hunt a man down for money—"

"That don't make no sense! Sheriffs and them other lawmen, they get paid for doing it."

"Part of their job—what they're hired to do."

"No difference that I can see. A outlaw is a outlaw, and who it is that brings him in oughtn't to bother nobody."

Starbuck's shoulders twitched. "Could be that regular lawmen usually try to keep a prisoner alive so's he can stand a trial, have a fair hearing in court. Bounty hunters aren't so particular—seem to prefer, in fact, to bring whoever they've caught in dead. Easier that way—you made that plain to me yourself."

"Can't see where that cuts any butter either. They're being hauled in to hang, and they're going to be dead, if the law does what it's supposed to, anyway—so what's the holler?"

"If you don't know," Shawn replied quietly, "there's not much chance of me making you see it."

"Maybe so, but right's right, and they earned what they've got coming, no matter how."

"And if a man's innocent—like me? What about him? What if you go ahead and do the executing yourself? That makes it murder and you're no better than any other killer."

"Always sure of what I'm doing. Just plain don't make no mistakes like that."

"You're making one now."

"And you're setting on that saddle, not hung across it—"

"But what if I made a run for it, tried to escape?"

"Reckon I'd have to kill you," Hillister said blandly.

"Which would make you a murderer in the same class as the killers you say you're after. How'd you explain it?"

The bounty hunter brushed his hat to the front of his head, scratched at the thick thatch covering it. "Why, I'd just say I had to do it, that's all. Was bringing you in and you tried to escape. Had to shoot."

"You think the law would let it go at that?"

"Sure. One man, more or less, don't mean nothing to them badge-toters. They'd figure you was guilty of something anyway, else you wouldn't have tried to run.

"You just don't understand how things is, Starbuck. It's mighty important that I keep hunting and bringing in killers and outlaws. Country's got to be shed of them so's decent folks'll be safe. You ought to understand that!"

Shawn fell silent. Being around Luke Hillister was like sitting on a powder keg while somebody played with lighted matches. The harsh, almost wild pitch of his voice, the fanatical gleam in his eyes made it clear that the slightest thing could set him off. He'd not argue with the man anymore; he'd wait, let Sheriff Trueman straighten him out.

Starbuck raised his head, looked beyond Hillister as they topped a low rise. A sigh slipped from his lips. The scatter of buildings in the hollow below would be Cimarron.

4 〜〜

Lambert's Saloon . . . DeBaca's Livery Stable . . . The St. James Hotel . . . Cimarron News & Press . . . Brick House Bar . . . N. Solomon, General Merchandise . . . Starbuck's glance idly ran down the street, as he ignored the interested stares of several persons moving along the sidewalks and of a group of blue-uniformed soldiers lounging in the shade of a cottonwood near the hotel. They'd be from Fort Union, he supposed.

He knew a man from Cimarron—or at least, had known. Allison his name was, a slim, limping gun-hawk who handled a weapon with amazing speed and deadly accuracy. They had met, united forces briefly in some trouble, and then parted. Allison had been sort of a leader in a range war that had raged in that part of New Mexico—something to do with a foreign-owned syndicate, the local ranchers, and a cattle king who had possessed at the time almost two million acres of prime land. Shawn wondered, as they drew up before the sheriff's office, if Allison was still around.

The soldiers and two or three other men began to drift toward the jail. Hillister, ignoring them, swung from his saddle, looped the reins around the hitchrack crossbar, and, hand resting on his pistol, turned to watch Starbuck, hampered by bound wrists, come off the sorrel.

As Shawn dropped to the ground, the bounty hunter caught him by the shoulder, shoved him roughly toward the open doorway of the lawman's quarters. Starbuck swore as anger flared through him, but he said nothing to Hillister, simply righted himself and entered the squat, adobe brick building.

Bart Trueman, a thin, gray man with a trailing mustache and small, beadlike eyes, was standing in the rear of the room, arms folded across his chest, legs apart. Leaning against the opposite wall was a short, skull-faced individual in rumpled business suit. A discussion had apparently been taking place between them, one interrupted by the bounty hunter and his prisoner.

Trueman waited until they had halted in front of the scarred table that served as a desk, and then nodded curtly to Hillister.

"Who's this?"

The bearded bounty hunter flicked a glance at the small crowd collected outside the doorway and said, "Claims his name's Starbuck. I figure him for a liar. . . . Want you to look him up," he added, dropping Shawn's pistol onto the table.

Starbuck felt the lawman's cold eyes rake him from head to toe. "That your real name, mister?"

"Same one I've had since I was born."

"You prove it?"

"If I have to," Shawn said.

Trueman was silent for a long moment and then moved up to the table. Reaching into a basket he took up a stack of printed reward posters, and sinking into a chair, began to go through them.

"Name don't ring no bell," he murmured.

"I'm betting it ain't his real one," Hillister said.

The sheriff paused, leveled his gaze at the bounty hunter. Anger was stirring him. "Then why the hell'd you bring him in if you don't know for sure who he is?"

Luke Hillister drew himself up stiffly. "Can see from looking at him that he's a bad one—wearing that gun low and tied down like he was—and it sure ain't brand new!" Raising his arm he pointed a thick finger at the weapon on the desk. "See for yourself, can't you?"

The man in the business suit pulled away from the wall, a look of amazement on his features. "You mean that's the reason you brought him in?" he asked in an incredulous tone.

The bounty hunter's eyes brightened. He clawed impatiently at his beard. Trueman glanced at the speaker, shook his head. "I'll handle this, Cameron," he said and continued to leaf through the stack of dodgers.

"That's him!" Hillister yelled suddenly, lunging forward and stabbing one of the posters with a forefinger. "Him, sure'n hell!"

The sheriff devoted a moment's study to the printed photograph on the sheet, shook his head, and leaned back. "Ain't him. This here's Buck Ward—and I know Buck."

"I'm telling you it's him!" Hillister shouted. "You just ain't wanting to jail him—and pay me my reward!"

Trueman raised his eyes to the crowd outside his office. The murmuring that had risen silenced immediately.

"Different man," he said and continued to go through the remainder of the posters. Finished, he stacked them between his fingers and dropped them back into the wire basket. "I got nothing on you, Starbuck."

"Knew that," Shawn said and extended his bound wrists. "Be obliged if you'll cut me loose."

"No—you ain't going to do that!" Hillister yelled, hand dropping to his pistol.

Bart Trueman's features froze as his eyes narrowed. He came to his feet slowly. "Don't give me any trouble, Hillister," he said in an icy voice. "You made a fool mistake this time. Admit it—and ride on out."

"You're just crooking me—"

"Get moving, Hillister—unless you want me to lock you up!"

The bounty hunter whirled angrily, eyes burning. "I'm going," he snarled, "but I ain't forgetting this! I ain't forgetting nothing!"

Shawn turned, watched the bounty hunter stamp heavily out of the room and cross to where his horse waited. A moment later he felt his wrists separate as the lawman cut the thongs binding him.

"Tried to tell him I was no outlaw," he said, facing Trueman. "Can give you the names of a few men who'll vouch for me if you're not sure. Nearest'll be Wyatt Earp in Dodge City."

The sheriff's eyes flickered. "Not necessary . . . You riding through or did something special bring you to Cimarron?"

"Was on my way to Santa Fe," Starbuck said, chafing his wrists to restore circlulation.

"And Hillister jumped you?"

"While I was making camp. At Cold Water Mountain. Tried to tell him—"

"Pretty hard to tell that jasper anything," Trueman said. "About half crazy. Pretty lucky for you he brought you in alive."

Shawn picked up his gun, dropped it into its holster. The crowd had dissipated, but the man called Cameron still leaned against the wall.

"How's it happen you let somebody like him run loose? Seems pretty dangerous."

"Reckon he is but there ain't nothing I can do about

it," the lawman said stiffly. "He ain't done nothing wrong—yet. If he does, and it happens in my county, I'll grab him quick."

"That'll be too late for the man he makes a mistake on. . . . He hang around here regularly?"

"Nope, just drifts back and forth all through the country—Colorado, Texas, Arizona—even far as California, I've heard. These parts mostly, however. Got a wife in a sanitarium somewhere around Denver."

"Sanitarium? Saw him looking at a picture of her and two boys. Was real touchy about it."

"Boys are dead—and she might as well be," Bart Trueman said, settling back in his chair. "That's what set old Luke Hillister off."

Starbuck frowned. "Figured there was something wrong with him. Met a few bounty hunters in my time but none of them like him. Seems to have a special hate on for all outlaws—more than's ordinary."

"Natural. Was because a bunch raided his farm one day—was back a few years ago. Caught his wife and boys. Killed them and done some mighty bad things to her. She lost her mind because of it.

"Reckon Luke sort of lost his, too, when he found them. Ended up with him putting her in that place near Denver and him starting out to catch—or kill—every outlaw he could get tabs on. Does it all legal. Hands them over to the nearest lawman he can find, collects his reward, and moves on. Found out from the sheriff up in Canyon City that he uses the money he gets to pay for his wife's keep."

"Told me he was saving to buy a place. Aims to make a home for her, I guess."

Trueman shrugged. "Ain't never heard about that. Just no figuring a man like him. He say where this place he's getting is?"

Starbuck shook his head. "Never mentioned it."

"Well, I'm hoping it ain't around here. Place is just healing up from the war we had. Can do without trouble for a spell—a long spell."

"Don't think you'll see the last of him—at least not right away. He's looking for two brothers. Was after them when he jumped me."

The lawman frowned, stroked his mustache. Cameron once again drew away from the wall.

"He say what their names were?"

"No—"

"It'll be the Kings," Cameron said, facing Trueman. "Can't be anybody else."

"Expect you're right, but they don't live in my county. Be up to somebody else to look after them."

"But you can't—"

Bart Trueman came to his feet, extended his hand to Shawn. "Right sorry Hillister put you through what he did. Sort of gives us a bad name."

"No fault of yours," Starbuck replied. "And speaking of names, I used to know a man from here. Was called Allison. He still around?"

The lawman's manner changed swiftly. He withdrew his hand, considered Shawn coldly.

"Clay Allison?"

"That's him. Like to pass the time of day—"

"Moved on—to Colorado," Trueman said flatly. "He a close friend of yours?"

"Guess you could say that. We swapped favors once."

"Well, he ain't here no more. . . . Expect you'll be moving on."

It was more a statement of fact than a question, and its implication was clear. Evidently friends of Clay Allison were unwelcome.

"Seems I am," Starbuck said dryly, and turned for the door. "Obliged to you for pulling that bounty hunter off my back."

Bart Trueman grunted indifferently. "Reckon it comes under the heading of being my job."

5 〜〜

Shawn stepped out into the sunlight, moved up to the sorrel at the hitchrack. He heard a sound behind him, turned. It was the man called Cameron.

"Like to have a word with you."

Starbuck smiled tightly, jerked his head at the sheriff's office. "Don't think the law wants me around any longer it takes me to mount up and ride."

Cameron frowned and then nodded as understanding came to him. "Oh, Clay Allison. Don't hold that against Bart. Truth is, Clay's a friend of his, but he's a man trouble just naturally dogs along with, and after all the hell that roared in and out of here during the range war, Bart'd as soon not have him or any of his kind in the county. This place was an armed camp for quite a while."

"Not sure I'm being complimented by being put in the same class as Allison or not, but from what I know of the man, I'd say I am. What did you want to talk about?"

"That crazy bastard of a Hillister and the Kings. Can we do it over a drink? I'm a mite dry."

Starbuck shrugged, said, "Why not?" and, freeing the sorrel's leathers, led him toward the rack at Lambert's Saloon. Anchoring the big horse there, he followed Cameron into the low-ceilinged, dark structure and sat down at a table in the corner.

The bartender stepped up, bringing a half-empty bottle, apparently Cameron's private stock, and two glasses, and turned away. Two men standing at the counter paused to watch and then also resumed their original positions.

Cameron poured drinks, lifted his, said *"Salud"* and tossed it off. Then, "Like to know what all it was Hillister said about the Kings."

"Don't know that it was the Kings he was talking about," Shawn replied, downing the liquor. "Only mentioned it was two brothers he was after."

Cameron nodded thoughtfully. "It's them, all right."

"They outlaws?"

"Guess you can say they were. Straight now far as I know."

Shawn considered the man quietly. "What's your interest in them? They some kin to you?"

The lean-faced man smiled, bobbed his head. "Guess Bart never did get around to introducing us, did he? I'm John Cameron. Came here from the east. Spot of lung trouble. Do a little newspaper writing for the press back there. Got interested in the Kings when they were having their trouble. Felt kind of sorry for them."

"They get it straightened out?"

"Far as the law was concerned. The two of them were sent to the pen a couple of years ago for a bank robbery in Colorado. Claimed they were innocent but the judge put them in anyway—ten years each. Then about a year ago they were turned loose—pardoned."

"Came out that they weren't guilty, that it?"

"Something like that, was never made exactly clear. It could've been there was no point keeping them locked up any longer. The younger of the two—Ollie—got worked over by a gang of other convicts one day. Ended up he'd been better off if they had killed him—shape they left him in. And I don't think the judge was ever dead sure in his own mind that Aaron, he's the other brother, was guilty in the first place. Anyhow, they were both pardoned."

"Then Hillister's making a mistake again—"

"Is as far as the law is concerned. What's worrying me is that Hillister being the kind of a crazy killer he is, he's liable to stir up some bad trouble."

Starbuck frowned. "Thing to do is catch up with him, make him understand the Kings aren't wanted by the law."

"Too late for that. He's gone—and you heard what

Bart Trueman said about it. The Kings don't live in this county, so it's not his problem. . . . Doubt if you could get Hillister to listen, anyway. The fact that the law pardoned them wouldn't mean a thing to him. He'd claim Ollie and Aaron were still outlaws and shouldn't have been turned loose—and he'll find a way to do his own executing."

"I can believe that. His mind runs in one groove. Why tell me about it?"

"I think the Kings ought to be warned—told to lay low until he moves on."

Shawn shook his head. "Don't think he's apt to do that."

Cameron swore wearily. "No, expect he won't. He's got his nose pointed at them and he won't back off until he's done something about what he thinks is a failure of the law to do what it should."

"Take it into his own hands, you mean?"

"Exactly, and I think the Kings ought to at least be warned so they can be ready."

A slow smile pulled at Starbuck's lips. "And you want me to be the one who warns them."

Cameron nodded. "You're headed that way, and with a little hard riding you could get in front of Hillister, beat him to the King place."

"Or maybe run smack into him doing it—"

"Good chance of that without going to the Kings. Expect you realize he's not through with you. He didn't believe what Bart Trueman told him, still figures you for a wanted outlaw. My guess is he'll be laying for you."

"Sort of got that idea myself."

"Well, if he does," John Cameron said, pouring himself another drink, "you'd better drop him before he can you because that's what he'll have in mind this time. He's got a hate bigger'n the whole Territory on for outlaws over this thing where he lost his boys, and he's out to avenge them whether the law's interested or not. Just happens that so far he's either killed or captured ones the law was after, so he's still in the clear."

"Appreciate the warning," Starbuck said. "Sort of had it figured that way—and I don't much like the idea of having to duck and dodge."

"Can't blame you there. Man's entitled to ride across country without fearing for his life. But there's one thing sure, if you meet up with him again, you'll have to kill him or he'll kill you."

Starbuck digested that quietly. After a time he brushed his hat back, said, "Could be what it'll come to, but it's something that'll have to be handled when I come to it."

"What about the Kings?"

"Don't like to get mixed up in things like this, but I guess something ought to be done. Hillister's a looney, or near to it, and I'd have trouble sleeping nights if I thought I'd let him walk in on them when I could've stopped it."

"Then you'll do it?"

Shawn nodded. "How do I get there?"

Cameron rubbed at his jaw. "Well, I don't exactly know. About a day's ride southeast is all I can tell you.

40

Just have to ask when you get down in that part of the country."

Starbuck sighed, got to his feet. "That being the way of it, I reckon I'd best get started," he said and extended his hand. "Pleasure meeting you."

"Same here," Cameron replied, taking Shawn's fingers into his own. "It's a mighty fine thing you're doing for those folks."

Starbuck bobbed his head and turned for the door. It seemed he was forever getting caught up in someone else's trouble, so much so in fact that at times he almost lost sight of his own purpose—that of finding Ben.

6 ~~~

A wry grin twisted Shawn Starbuck's lips as he rode south out of Cimarron. In all the days and months he'd spent and the miles of trail he'd covered in search of his brother, he'd never been taken for an outlaw and hauled in before a sheriff.

There had been a couple of times when something akin to that had occurred, but being tied up, planted on his horse, and led in at the end of a rope was a new experience. He'd have a few things to tell Ben about what he'd gone through during the quest, once he found him.

If ever he did.

Shawn's weather-tempered features sobered as that amending thought came to him. It was true—there seemed to be no end to the search. He had cut back and forth across the frontier innumerable times, all to no avail. Ben was not to be found. Often he had come close, or seemed to, and that likely was the spur that kept him going—the prospect that his brother was nearby, could very possibly be in the next town he rode into.

But disappointment was always his reward and there came moments when he thought such was fated to be the case forever, and a pressing urge to forget it, to forsake all hope of locating Ben and settling old Hiram's estate would enter his mind.

He could spend his lifetime at the task; he could fritter away all opportunity for a home, the ranch he planned one day to own, the wife and family he'd like to have—and still come out loser. All too often this occurred to him, nagged at his consciousness; but in the end he doggedly moved on, continued the search, driven by some inner voice that told him it was right, that it must be done—an obligation he could not shirk.

Now, shading his eyes with a cupped hand, he stared across the gently rolling land that stretched before him. It was far removed from the farm along the Muskingum River, yet there was something about the scene that evoked memories of his distant home. The grass, turning now with the approach of the cold months, looked much the same as it carpeted the slopes and small valleys; and the trees, perhaps it was the trees, cottonwoods and not tall sycamores to be sure, but great, spreading friends nevertheless.

The Starbuck farm had been a fine one and growing up there had been good, a time of many pleasures and joys despite the unbending strictness of their father. He and Ben, seven years his senior, had whiled away countless hours playing in the fields, fishing for punkin-seed perch in a nearby pond, or simply lying in the shade along the river dreaming aloud of the day when they would be men and go out into the world and do the things that fired their imaginations. . . . There had always been time for dreams although the chores that awaited them often seemed endless.

Chores—that was what had caused the break between Ben and their parent. Since he was the older of the two sons, Ben naturally assumed a larger share of the labor around the place than Shawn, and punishment visited upon him one day for a job neglected was what broke the dam of resentment.

It likely would have never occurred had Clare, their mother, still been alive. An understanding, educated woman, she was the reasoning and leveling force between her husband and their sons. When she died from a midwinter siege of lung fever, the prelude to the end of the family was signaled.

Hiram, a squat bull of a man skilled in the arts of both scientific boxing and practical farming, turned inward. His bitterness at losing the quiet, gray-eyed woman he worshiped settled upon his older son, who endured it for a time, and then in a frenzy of anger, renounced all kinship with his father and took his leave.

Shawn stayed on, living with his father in a relationship that heretofore he had not known, bearing the man's moods silently, applying himself to the teachings of old Hiram, and generally making the best of it all.

When his father died, leaving the farm and a sizable amount of cash as an estate, he accepted the terms of the will—that he first find Ben and return him to Muskingum before it would be settled—without question or rancor. Equipping himself as best he could on a small loan advanced by the administrator of the estate, he set out on what he had assumed at the start would be a simple task. Ben had often said he would like to go to Texas, join with a family there that had earlier made the move.

It had been Shawn's first stopping point, and initial disappointment. Ben had been there, tarried for a time, and ridden on.

Thus the search began, an endless trek punctuated by jobs taken periodically to obtain cash that would enable him to press on further to the next town—the next ranch—to anywhere where a man answering the meager description of his brother might be.

But Ben, if it were Ben, was never there; only the disheartening possibility that it could have been, and once more he would take to the saddle, move on while the transition from farm boy to cool-eyed, efficient trail rider, capable in all the skills of holding his own and staying alive in a world of violence steadily made itself more apparent.

The vast, sprawling land slumbering in the shadow of the Sangre de Cristo Mountains was empty. If Luke Hillister was somewhere ahead, he was taking pains to remain well hidden. Starbuck rubbed at the stubble on his cheeks, reached back into his mind to recall what he could about the country he had earlier crossed with the bounty hunter.

If Hillister planned an ambush, and it seemed logical, he most likely would set it in the rough, broken butte country still some distance ahead. Shawn glanced to the west; two hours or more of daylight left. Luke was timing it about right for him. He would be drawing near the bluffs around dark.

He hoped he could avoid the man, not come to a showdown with him. He had no real reason to shoot it out, to kill him, but he was fully aware that he could be faced with no choice. Hillister was bordering on total madness, wholly dangerous, and Starbuck knew he could not afford to let himself be taken captive again.

Again he swept the country with eyes half closed to cut down the glare; nothing in sight except a few larks dipping and curving as they skimmed above the grass. Easing back on the saddle, he allowed the sorrel to continue its steady lope.

A time later he came to the edge of the ragged, deeper-lying land. It was an area of short palisades, arroyos, and rocks tumbled recklessly to all quarters. He slowed the gelding, proceeded quietly.

Abruptly he came to a full stop. A trailing clump of brush growing at the end of a low butte caught his attention. He had seen no motion, no shadow, but instinct had stirred him, set up a hurried warning. He studied the rough-faced shoulder intently for several minutes and then glancing to the slope on his right, he cut the sorrel about and began to ascend it.

7 ~~~

There was no trail up the steep grade but Starbuck kept the sorrel climbing and after a bit, reached a fairly level bench that paralleled the road below. Dismounting to lower the silhouette, he took up the gelding's reins and stepped out in front of him, moving quietly and carefully.

He drew abreast the back of the low bluff with its beard of brush, halted. Leaving the sorrel ground reined, Shawn dropped to hands and knees and worked his way to the rim of the ledge. Brushing off his hat, he peered down into the arroyo.

Hillister was there. The bounty hunter had stationed himself in the center of the undergrowth after first concealing his horse farther back, and now stood, gun in hand, awaiting the arrival of his intended prisoner.

That he had been seen coming was evident to Starbuck as he lay motionless on the rocky shelf and studied the man. Hillister was set, ready to strike; and it was equally obvious his intentions were not to bother with taking his victim in alive this time.

A tight grin tugged at Starbuck's mouth. If he hadn't spotted the brush clump at the edge of the bluff when he did and obeyed the subconscious warning it had stirred to life within him, he would, in all likelihood at that moment be slung head down across his saddle and on his way to some lawman different from Bart Trueman who Hillister felt would be more receptive.

He pulled back, retraced his steps to the sorrel, his glance raking the slope on ahead as he crossed over. The ledge flattened into the grade and disappeared entirely a short distance on. The point was well below Luke Hillister but whether he could remain unseen during the final span and the subsequent descent to the road below, as well as go unheard, was problematical.

No other course was open to him. Doubling back would be risky and he would be facing the same danger of being seen and heard. Nor was waiting for full darkness an answer; it would be difficult enough negotiating the steep slope without the added problem of night obscuring his way.

He swore softly, irked at being forced to take such precautions to avoid the man—any man. It rubbed him wrong and he rebelled at the need, but he pushed his pride into the background; it was either that or run head-on into Luke Hillister and a gunfight in which he would either kill the man or himself be killed—all for no good purpose.

Gathering up the sorrel's reins, he continued along the narrowing ledge. Several times the horse's iron-shod hooves clicked against rock, caused him to halt abruptly, wait out a long, tense minute until he was certain he had not roused the bounty hunter's suspicions.

Even then he was not completely sure; he could no longer see the man, could only listen, and, hearing nothing, believe his movements had gone unnoticed.

The shelf began to fade, dissolve into a slight, rolling hump and finally disappear into the hillside entirely. Starbuck paused there, debating the advisability of pursuing his present course of action or of simply mounting the sorrel, giving him his head and making a rapid, and undoubtedly noisy descent.

It would put Hillister on his trail instantly, and he had no liking for that thought. He faced a tedious job of locating the King place and passing the warning to them as it was without having the very person he would caution them about dogging his heels.

Best stick with his present plan, take the horse down slow, walking ahead of him, crowding him back hard to prevent him from breaking into a series of stiff-legged jumps that would set up a sure-to-be-heard racket. He'd need to be careful, however; the big gelding could get off balance, and, unable to stop, come down upon him.

Taking the sorrel's cheek strap in his hand, Starbuck started down the slope, moving in small steps, following a long tangent in an effort to cut down on the steepness. At once small cascades of dirt and gravel began to pour from under the sorrel's hooves, rattling hollowly over the rocks. Starbuck did not pause; there was no time to wait, only hope he was far enough beyond Luke Hillister for it to go unheard.

He reached the foot of the slope, halted, breathing

hard from the effort of steadying the trembling sorrel. Mounting at once, he moved out of the small cluster of cedars at the base of the grade, and, keeping to the soft ground to deaden the sorrel's hoofbeats, angled for the road.

Movement to his left brought him up sharp. The towering shape of Luke Hillister, gun in hand, stepped from behind the thickly branched trees. Starbuck threw himself forward on the saddle, drove his spurs brutally into the flanks of the gelding, sent him lunging straight at the bounty hunter—it was too late for anything else.

The pistol in Hillister's grasp blasted echoes into the late afternoon hush. Starbuck felt the breath of a bullet as the shoulder of his shying horse grazed the man, knocked him backwards into the cedars. Veering sharp right, he raced on, glancing over his shoulder as the sorrel gained the road, began to pound along its hard, worn surface. There was no sign of Luke Hillister. He apparently still lay unconscious in the scrubby growth.

Shawn did not slacken the gelding's pace until full dark and then pulled off into a wide arroyo that came into the trail from the left. Choosing a spot high on the lower side that would enable him to see anyone entering the wash and also permit him to move on if the need arose, without being noticed, he made dry camp. He had shaken Hillister, he felt certain, but he took no chances and passed up his need for coffee since it would require a fire, and made a meal of cold biscuits, dried beef, canned peaches, and water from his canteen.

His needs and those of the sorrel satisfied, he climbed to the top of a nearby hill for a look at his back trail. By following the now dark rim of the bluffs along which he had made his way he was able to ascertain the approximate point where Luke Hillister had laid his ambush.

He studied the area for some time but for all his careful probing he could not detect a campfire; either the bounty hunter was being as cautious as he or else, once recovered from the hard blow he had taken, had mounted his horse and followed. Understanding Hillister's devious mind, the latter appeared the most likely to Starbuck, but he shrugged off the possibility as of no consequence.

The graveled floor of the arroyo would show no indication of his turning off and he was well hidden far back from the road. The sorrel had weathered a hard day and he was equally tired. Grim, he returned to camp, rolled up in his blanket, and dropped off to sleep. He would run no farther.

Daylight, crisp and bone chilling, roused him. Again passing up the genuine need for a fire and the warmth it would provide as well as the hot breakfast it would make possible, he rode out immediately, slanting the sorrel due southeast into the area where John Cameron had told him the Kings lived.

By midmorning the sun had broken the chill, and as periodic glances behind him failed to note a following horseman, he pulled into a deep wash to prepare and eat the breakfast he had passed up earlier.

Finished, he again went to the saddle, feeling much better and certain now he had thrown Hillister off his trail. He could ease off, look for someone who could direct him to the King ranch, or homestead, whichever it was; likely he was drawing near to it.

It was full noon, however, when he finally came upon a rider hazing a jag of steers along the bed of a sandy wash. Shawn swung up to the man at once, a squat, slack-jowled individual in worn range clothing and run-down boots who viewed him with cold suspicion.

Starbuck passed the usual salutations, then asked: "Know a family around here named King?"

The puncher stared at him woodenly. "Maybe."

"You a friend of theirs?"

The cowhand shifted on the misshapen saddle he was forking. The horn had been broken off and the whole thing appeared to be held together with rawhide cord and baling wire.

"Reckon there ain't nobody can claim to be real friendly with them," he drawled and spat into the sand.

"But I guess you know them—"

"Ain't saying I don't."

"I've got an important message for them," Starbuck said. "Mind telling me how to find their place?"

"You a stranger around here?"

Shawn nodded, the point seeming to be self-evident to him.

"Well, I don't know," the puncher said, wagging his head. "You sure that's why you're wanting to see them?"

"The only reason. . . . Their ranch on to the south, or the east?"

The cowhand shifted on his creaky hull, lifting himself slightly in an evident precaution against getting himself pinched, and pointed to a long line of dark-shadowed hills.

"Can't say as it's a ranch, but the Kings've got a place 'round the end of them bluffs. You just keep heading the way you are and you'll run smack dab into it."

"Obliged to you," Starbuck said, nodding. "One thing more—if you come across a big, black-bearded man asking you the same question, you'll be doing the Kings a favor if you tell him you don't know."

The puncher considered Shawn with expressionless eyes, his slack mouth half open. After a few moments he shrugged. "I'll study on it," he said laconically, and slapping heels against the old gray he was riding, moved on.

8 ~~~

Starbuck drew up at the end point of the palisades and let his gaze run the scatter of buildings in the small valley below. . . . The King place. He shook his head.

It was a scene of near desolation. The main house, of logs, was gray and sagged from time and weather. Beyond it stood a barn, its bulk canted slightly to one side as if braving the wind. Nearby was a wagon shed, the roof of which drooped to the ground at its lower end, three or four crumbling minor structures, and a rotting, pole corral reinforced along its base to contain a flock of chickens. There was a small shack, a bit apart, where someone had planted morning glories along the walls in a pitiful attempt to soften the bleakness.

The area fronting the buildings had been cleared for a considerable distance, leaving the soil barren and baked hard by the sun, but in the rear, besides clumps of brush, Shawn could see the green oblong of a garden in which grew corn and other vegetables.

After a time Starbuck touched the sorrel with his rowels and rode down the slope toward the structures. He proceeded at slow pace and kept as much in the open as possible, not in the least interested in drawing a bullet intended for an intruder.

When he reached the edge of the brush that fringed the yard, he again halted. He hoped that someone in the house would have seen him by that moment and stepped into the open to challenge his arrival; it would have given him a more comfortable feeling. But there were no signs of life and the thought came to him that the place was deserted, that the Kings had moved on. . . . Still, there were chickens in their improvised pen, and the garden looked to be well tended.

Staying within the encroaching brush, Starbuck began to work in nearer, following the circle of rank growth to where he could attain a position close to the main house. He halted abruptly. There had been movement behind one of the windows. There was definitely someone inside—and that they had seen him was also certain.

Shawn felt the hair on the back of his neck crawl. There was no welcome here for him—not for anyone, he guessed. The Kings, having had their troubles with the outside world, had become hostile and wary of all strangers.

He was as near as it was prudent, he decided, and cupping his hand to his mouth, shouted: "Hello—the house!"

There was no response. He waited out a long minute, repeated the call. Again there was fleeting movement beyond the dusty, streaked glass of the window next to the door. Starbuck swore impatiently. He'd have to simply ride in, hope for the best. . . . At least it would be no surprise to them; they knew he was there.

"Climb down off that horse!"

Shawn stiffened at the sharp command. He started to turn, froze as the harsh, high-pitched voice struck at him once more.

"You hear? Climb down—and don't go reaching for no gun, or by God, I'll blow your head off!"

Raising one hand and grasping the saddle horn with the other, Starbuck swung from the sorrel. Feet on the ground, both arms now up, he wheeled slowly. Surprise rolled through him.

He faced a woman. Stringy, red hair streaked with gray, leathery face set, pale blue eyes snapping, she considered him with unmistakable hatred. Somewhere in her late fifties, she was dressed in a man's faded and patched shirt, baggy pants that were too large, and heavy, thick-soled sodbuster shoes.

She had tied an apron around her waist, had gathered the two lower corners to form a basket in which she had placed several ears of corn, a few tomatoes, and onion. Likely she was the woman of the King clan and he had interrupted her while she gathered vegetables for the table.

But there was no motherliness in the manner in which she held an old Navy Colt. The hammer was drawn back and she held it leveled steadily at Starbuck's belly. That she had used it before and would do so again was apparent.

"Mean you no harm," he said, shaking his head.

"You're a goddam liar—and a spy, that's what," the woman snapped. "One of Harper's bunch, come here to try and trick us. Well, you ain't fooling me none!"

"Never heard of Harper—"

"Don't try lying to me! I've been watching you, sneaking through the brush. We know the whole lot of you're setting back there in the hills, waiting and hoping for the time when you could catch us not looking."

"Not with anybody," Starbuck said patiently. "I'm alone."

"Sure you are—same as I'm the queen of England! Move on ahead of me—and keep your hands up."

"Where—"

"To the house—where the hell else you think I'd take you? I'm keeping you a prisoner—a hostage. Maybe I can make that Chet Harper come to terms, does he find

55

out I got one of his bunch hogtied and ready for slaughtering."

"You're all wrong, Mrs. King—if that's who you are—"

"You know goddamn well I'm Ma King! Move—start for the house—straight! You try something cute and you'll be deader'n a stuffed owl!"

Starbuck pushed forward through the waist-high brush, taking slow, careful steps and broke out onto the cleared ground. Halfway to the house Ma King jabbed him savagely in the spine with her pistol.

"Hold up right there," she barked, and pointing her weapon at the sky, triggered a shot that roused a rolling chain of echoes.

"Want Harper for sure to see I've got you," she said, her brittle blue eyes looking beyond Shawn to the low hills several hundred yards to the west.

He followed her gaze. A half a dozen riders were gathered on the crest of the highest, were facing the yard, watching.

"Reckon that'll do it," Ma King said, and shifted her attention to the house. "Aaron, open the door!"

The hewn plank panel swung inward. The woman again jabbed Starbuck with her pistol. "All right, get inside—and no foolishness if you're of a mind to keep on living! . . . Get his gun, Aaron."

As Shawn stepped through the doorway into the dim, cluttered structure, a man, also redheaded and blue-eyed, closed in behind him, deftly lifted his weapon from its holster, and pulled back.

"Who's he?"

"One of Harper's bunch sent down here to spy on us," the woman replied, kicking the door shut with her heel. "Expecting they're getting ready for another try."

"You're all wrong," Starbuck began. "I'm—"

"Keep your gun pointing at him while I dump these vittles," the woman directed, circling toward a crude table built against the wall near the cookstove. "Then we'll tie him up. Maybe Harper'll hold off now that we've got one of his'n."

"Doubt it," Aaron replied, motioning Shawn toward a cowhide chair with the muzzle of the pistol he held.

Starbuck sat down, wondering as he did where the other brother might be. Apparently Ma King was a widow, had been forced to take over as head of the family years ago, and in the process had become as hard-minded and iron-fisted as her husband had probably been.

He watched her lay the old Navy Colt on the table and unload her apron. That done, she jerked at the strings tied about her middle, released the ankle-length square of calico, and hung it on a wall peg. Turning, she then rummaged about in a box under the table and produced a short length of rope.

"This here'll hold him," she said, and, crossing to where Starbuck sat, pulled his wrists behind him and lashed them securely together. As an added precaution she used the trailing end of the cord to bind his ankles.

"Want you to listen to me," Shawn said as she straightened up. "I came here to do you a favor—"

"You come here to spy on us," Ma King broke in, striding to the window near the door. "Harper sent you to watch, see if there was a way he could get inside, once we holed up, without getting his danged hide blasted!"

"No, you're wrong. I—"

"Well, we're a jump ahead of him now! He tries anything, we got you to dicker with," the woman said, peering through the glass. "If he wants to keep you alive, he'll back off, leave us be."

Shawn stirred in frustration. "I'm telling you I've got nothing to do with somebody named Harper! Just rode by to warn you about—"

"They're coming," Ma King said, paying no attention to Starbuck's words. "You get over there to the other window, Aaron—and make your shooting count. We ain't long on bullets."

"Yes, Ma," King said and hurriedly crossed to the opening on the other side of the door.

The woman, hitching at the gun belt she was wearing and which had gone unnoticed under her apron, stationed herself beside the cracked panes in the sash. Raising it slightly, she paused, turned half about, and swept the cabin with a frowning glance. Outside, Shawn could hear the quick pound of approaching horses.

"Where's Ollie?"

The surprise in Ma King's voice indicated that in the excitement of capturing a prisoner she had not noticed the absence of the rest of her family.

"Him and Dora went down to the shack," Aaron replied, and then ducked back as bullets began to thud into the log walls of the house and the rattle of gunshots filled the yard.

9 ~~~

"Goddammit!" Ma King said feelingly, "I told them to stay inside while Harper was hanging around."

Aaron rested the barrel of his rifle on the window's sill and pressed off a shot. He handled the weapon with an awkwardness that bordered on timidity.

"Went to get something—something Dora wanted," he said. "Aimed to be gone only a minute."

"She'll fool around and get Ollie and herself killed, that's what she's going to get," the woman snapped, opening up with her pistol.

The shooting outside was a continuous racket and a steady hail of bullets hammered at the thick walls and heavy door of the cabin. Glass shattered suddenly and Ma King jerked back, swearing lustily.

She brushed at the tip of her nose with the back of a hand. "We ain't hit a one of them yet! Guess I just can't set my mind to it with Ollie and Dora caught out there like they are. . . . Bet they didn't even take no gun with them."

Aaron shook his head. "Don't recollect," he said glancing around the room. "Didn't take the shotgun 'cause there it is. And Pa's rifle's laying on the bench."

"That Dora Clark ain't got a lick of sense! If that

Harper bunch finds out they're trapped in the shack, they'll damn quick—"

Ma King's voice faded as she turned, resumed firing at the marauders. Starbuck glanced around the cabin; small, skimpily furnished with crudely built furniture, it was scarcely more than one room. A partition had been erected in the south corner to form a bedroom, used, no doubt by Ma herself. Adjacent to it and on the same wall a double bunk had been built—serving as sleeping facilities for Ollie and Aaron. The opposite, rear corner was devoted to kitchen use. Where Dora, the girl mentioned, fit into the scheme and who she was Shawn had no way of knowing.

Glass tinkled again and through the thin haze of smoke that was beginning to fill the cabin, Starbuck saw Aaron draw back, look down at his left wrist where flying splinters had drawn blood.

"Don't know what this is all about, but if you'll turn me loose I'll give you a hand."

Aaron, injury forgotten and now taking the opportunity to reload, flicked a glance to his mother who made a negative gesture with her head.

"You can use another gun—"

King did not bother to look up but continued to feed cartridges into the magazine of his rifle.

"There's a half a dozen of them out there, and only two of you," Shawn continued. "They're going to realize that and when they do, they'll rush you."

Ma King wheeled angrily. "Mister, you're doing a lot of gabbling for nothing. Smart thing for you to do is shut your jaws until time comes for to figure out what I'm doing with you."

"Make him go get Dora and Ollie," Aaron suggested, stepping up to the window again. "Him a-walking with them'll keep Harper's bunch from shooting."

Ma King's eyes sharpened and a half smile pulled at her thin lips. "Now, that's a right smart idea, Aaron! They sure won't cut down on them with him right there in the way. You listening, mister?"

Starbuck shook his head. "Be a mistake. They don't know me. Be the same as one of you going out there."

Ma stared at him. "Can't you do nothing else but lie? Told you I wasn't swallowing that hogwash."

"Not lying—and if you're smart you'll listen to me. I'm not—"

"They're drawing back," Aaron announced through the acrid fog. "Reckon they're aiming to do some palavering—likely with this jasper, only he won't be showing up for the meeting."

The gunshots had ceased. Ma King, again reloading, stepped back into the room and took up a stand near Shawn.

"Turn him loose," she said, ducking her head at Aaron.

King propped his rifle against the wall and crossed to where Shawn sat. Leaning over, he began to fumble with the knots in the rope.

"You sending him after Dora and Ollie now?"

"Be a good time," the woman said. She waited until Starbuck was free and then, holding her pistol on him, beckoned him to the window. "You see that there little house at the end of the yard?" she asked, pointing.

Shawn looked through the jagged glass. It was the shack with the morning glories. He nodded.

"Well, here's the word with the bark still on it: you're stepping out that door and making a beeline for it. My boy and his girl are in there. You're bringing them back to me. That plain?"

"Plain enough but if you think I can do it without getting myself or them shot, you're loco," Shawn said bluntly.

Ma studied him with cold eyes. "I'm saying you can. Your friends ain't going to throw no lead at you."

"Not my friends—"

"All the time you're there in the yard me and Aaron'll have our guns pointing at you. Try running off and we'll fill you so full of bullets you'll weigh a ton. There ain't no place you can reach, once you're out there that we can't cut you down before you can get to it. You listening good?"

Starbuck shrugged wearily. It was useless to argue with the Kings, make them understand that he had no connection with the man they called Harper and his gang. Perhaps, if he could manage to cross the yard, gain the shack and return with Ollie and the girl, Dora, he might be able to convince them he was telling the truth. . . . But by doing so safely wouldn't he be proving their contention? He stirred again, realizing he was caught between a rock and a hard place.

"Now, when you start back with them, you keep them

to the inside. That way it'll be you walking betwixt them and your partners. You got that straight, too?"

"Won't make any difference. I'll look the same to Harper as your boy and this Dora."

"Don't forget what I told you now!" Ma King said, completely ignoring his words. "Try skinning out on me and you're a dead outlaw—hear?"

"I hear—"

The woman bucked her head at Aaron. "All right, open the door and let him out. I got to be standing here at the window so's I can hold a bead on him."

Shawn stepped up to the thick panel, halted. Anger and impatience were running through him at his failure to break down Ma King's stubbornness and make her hear what he had to say.

"Came by here to do you a favor," he said, deciding to make one more attempt. "Man named Cameron, up in Cimarron, wanted me to warn you—"

"Don't know no Cameron," she said, not taking her eyes from the yard. Evidently she was watching Harper and the riders with him, all of whom had pulled off to one side.

"He's a newspaper writer. Knows about you from the trouble your boys had with the law. Felt sorry for—"

"Ain't no need for nobody to feel sorry for us," Ma snapped. "Us Kings can look after ourselves. Always have, reckon we always will."

Shawn flinched as Aaron's rifle barrel pressed into his ribs, prodded him toward the door. He took a step nearer, halted, faced the woman.

"Can see that but the fact is there's a bounty hunter, name of Hillister, headed this way."

"Never heard of no Hillister either."

"He's after Aaron and Ollie—"

"Reckon we can handle him, too, was you to be telling the truth and he showed up. Now, goddammit, are you getting out there or am I going to have to wing you right here and now? I'm tired of you stalling."

Shawn swept Ma King with a look of disgust, swore under his breath, and reached for the door latch. Raising it, he drew in the slab panel and glanced out. Harper and the others were in the tall brush beyond the yard and well out of range.

He shifted his glance to the shack at the end of the barren yard to his left. There was no available cover; the moment he stepped out onto the hardpack, he was in the open.

"Start moving," he heard Ma King say, and, taking a deep breath, he darted through the doorway and ran hard for the shack.

10 ～～～

A faint yell went up as Starbuck legged it for the shack, but there were no gunshots. The distance was too great and shooting at him would be useless, but he knew that was not the way Ma King would see it; she would take it as proof that he was a member of Harper's gang and they had purposely withheld their fire.

He gained the small building, rushed through the door

that swung wide to admit him. Closing it, he glanced at the young woman—only a girl in fact—standing in the center of the room. She was pretty in a quiet sort of way—even, tanned features, honey-blonde hair and level gray eyes that considered him gravely.

"Who're you?" she asked, her expression not changing.

"Name's Starbuck. Ma King thinks I'm one of the Harper bunch. I'm not but there's no making her believe it. . . . She sent me to get you and Ollie."

He looked beyond the girl to the man, one little older than himself, sitting at a table in a corner. He had the same red hair and blue eyes as his mother and brother, only there was an emptiness to him, a vacancy as if there was nothing behind the facade of family similarity.

Shawn recalled what he had been told of Ollie King, that he had been set upon by other convicts while in prison and severely beaten; it would have been better had they killed him, so John Cameron had said. He understood those words now; Ollie was a mindless imbecile staring out at a world in which he did not live but merely existed as a helpless vegetable.

"Can he understand what you tell him?" he asked, returning his glance to Dora.

She nodded. "Sometimes."

"Then explain that we've got to make a run for the house. Ma and Aaron will give us cover, but we'll be taking a chance if Harper and the others with him open up on us."

Dora frowned, touched the empty holster on his hip with her eyes. "Don't you have a gun?"

Shawn grinned wryly. "Ma won't let me have one. Like I said, she figures I'm one of the gang."

"You're not?"

"No, and I'd sure as hell like to find a way to prove it. . . . We've got to hurry—Harper and his boys could be moving in."

Wheeling, he stepped to the door, opened it a narrow crack. The outlaws had moved forward but were still in the brush. They appeared to be watching the shack, evidently unsure as to what was going on. He shifted his eyes to the house. Ma King, at the window, was beckoning angrily.

He swung back to Dora and Ollie. The younger King's face. was slack, wooden, as he stared straight ahead. The girl nodded.

"I think he understands."

"Good. Once we're out there, run for the house fast as you can. I'll be on the outside, between you and Harper."

Dora's lips parted in a wan smile. She seemed curiously unafraid, considering the danger that lay ahead. "That sounds like Ma's doings, too—"

"Was. She gave me strict orders and I'm not about to buck her."

"I know what you mean. I've been around her for quite a spell now. Nobody's got the spunk to stand up to Ma."

Shawn again turned to the door, drew it partly open.

The outlaws—he realized in that moment that he was thinking of them in that sense simply because Ma King had labeled them as such; they could be just ordinary citizens, or possibly even lawmen—were moving toward the yard. He swore softly. They had waited too long.

Taut, he stepped back, jerked the panel wide. "Let's go," he said. "Don't stop until you're in the house!"

Dora, hanging tight onto Ollie's hand, hurried into the yard, veered at once toward the cabin. Starbuck rushed to her side, and together the three of them ran for the squat structure at the opposite end of the clearing.

"Come on, Ollie—race me!" he heard the girl cry.

King laughed childishly, increased his speed. Over to the left gunfire broke out. Shawn threw his attention to that point. Harper and his men were spurring out of the brush, breaking onto the hardpack and firing as they came.

Gunshots began to crackle from the windows of the house as Ma King and Aaron laid down a covering barrage. The approaching riders, free of the hindering undergrowth, began to close in fast. Dust spurted around Starbuck's feet as bullets drove into the sunbaked soil, thunked dully into the dead stumps of trees beyond them.

But suddenly they were at the house, plunging through the door held open by Aaron. Sucking hard for wind, Starbuck whirled, hearing the loud pound of hooves in the yard only moments behind them.

He saw Aaron rush back to his place at the window, realized that Ma King's weapon had gone empty and the resulting lack of return fire was allowing the outlaws to come in dangerously close.

Snatching up his pistol from the table where Aaron had laid it, he crossed quickly to the window. Grasping Ma by the shoulders, he lifted her out of the way.

"Excuse me, ma'am," he said, and, crowding up to the opening, began to add his shots to those of Aaron.

"One's hit!" the older King brother sang out, looking over his shoulder at Shawn. "Your first bullet got one!"

Starbuck watched the sagging rider wheel away, leveled on the man behind him, and pressed off another shot. The outlaw yelled, clawed at his arm, and cut back for the brush.

"Another'n!" Aaron yelled. "Was the one they call Tex." He came fully around, grinned broadly at his mother. "Reckon they'll start thinking twice about us now, Ma."

Shawn faced about. The elderly woman, pistol now in the holster belted around her waist, was watching him. A soft, wondering look was filling her eyes. Beyond her Ollie sat numbly in the same leather chair that earlier had confined Starbuck. Dora, an old double-barreled shotgun in her hands, was crossing to the window where Aaron stood.

"Expect they'll make their big try now," he said. "Best we all get set to open up on them. . . . They find out there's more than just two guns against them, they'll likely back off—maybe for good."

Ma King broke out of her absorption. "You heard him," she said briskly. "Dora, you stay there with Aaron. Me and the stranger'll stand them off from this here window."

Shawn, his weapon reloaded, drew to one side of the opening, making room for the matriarchal head of the King clan.

"They're coming!" Aaron cried.

The cabin rocked with the blast of the shotgun and other weapons. Harper, sided by only three riders, slowed in the face of the murderous volley. At once the men with him swerved to the side, began to pull away. The outlaw leader, suddenly alone in the yard, yelled something, flinched as a bullet tore at the brim of his hat. Abruptly he wheeled and spurred off in pursuit of his followers.

"I reckon that's it," Aaron said, his voice filled with satisfaction. "They ain't going to try that again."

Starbuck turned, began to thumb fresh cartridges into the cylinder of his forty-five. Squinting through the acrid smoke haze, he touched each of the others with his glance.

"Maybe not, but just in case they do, I'd like to know first why I'm doing all this shooting."

11 ~~~

In the sudden hush that settled over the room, Starbuck dropped his pistol back into its holster and leaned against the wall.

Dora, eyes upon him, did not move, simply watched and waited. Aaron lowered his head, began to refill the magazine of the rifle while his younger brother, a wooden image in the cowhide chair, stared blankly into space. Only Ma King stirred. Folding her arms she met Shawn's gaze coolly.

"Maybe it'd be best was you to catch up your horse and ride on," she said. "Wouldn't be right dragging you into our trouble."

"Seems I'm already in it," Starbuck said, shrugging.

"You come in it of your own wanting—and I'm saying now I was wrong about you, and I'm saying, too, I'm sorry. And I'm thanking you for pitching in like you did—but there ain't no call for your staying around now."

Shawn studied the older woman. Her words were coming only from the surface, born of a strange mixture of pride and politeness. Inwardly she was hoping that he would not go.

"Never like to start a job I don't finish," he said. "Who's this Harper?"

He could see relief flood through both Ma King and Dora at his question. Aaron heaved a sigh, continued to work with his weapon.

"Outlaw," Ma said. "Him and the bunch with him are all outlaws. Expect there's sheriffs and marshals looking for the whole passel, but they're plenty smart. Keep to the hills. . . . Rode in here about a week ago."

"Harper the only one you know?"

"Know them all," the woman said.

Turning, she took a leather pouch and a cob pipe from a shelf on the wall. Opening the sack, she pinched out a small quantity of the shredded leaves, began to tamp into the blackened bowl.

"Yessir, we know them all," she continued, digging into her shirt pocket for a match. "Paid us a visit here one day, bold as brass. There's one they call Dave Dismukes, and a Mexican—Gonzales. Another'n goes by the name of Tex Wingate—"

"He ain't liable to come again," Aaron broke in. "The stranger there winged him good."

"I'm called Starbuck," Shawn said.

"Then there's the one going by the handle, Georgia, a southern-talking fellow. Last one's Bill Drake—"

"Starbuck put a bullet in him, too, leastwise I think he's the one," Aaron cut in again.

"What do they want from you?" Shawn asked after a brief time, voicing the question that had been on his mind from the beginning. He could see nothing the Kings possessed that would warrant six men risking their lives to get.

Ma scratched a match into fire, held it to her pipe and puffed its contents into a glowing coal. Exhaling a cloud of smoke, she looked directly at him.

"Fifty thousand dollars."

Starbuck's jaw sagged. "Fifty thousand dollars! How —why—"

"They figure my boys knows where it's been hid. Was taken in a Wells-Fargo holdup."

Starbuck thought back, recalled what he'd heard in Cimarron about the King brothers and the reason why they had been sent to prison.

"Do they?"

"Hell no, they don't! Had nothing to do with it."

Shawn smiled. "Not what the law says."

The older woman glanced at him sharply. "You know something about it?"

"Was told Aaron and Ollie went to jail for a robbery. They spent a year of their sentence and then was pardoned. . . . Harper and his bunch must figure it's true, too, else they wouldn't be trying to find out about the money."

"Only guessing. Showed up here first time, nice and friendly as you please—but they was feeling us out all along. Could see that. Then when we didn't tell them nothing because we couldn't, they started getting nasty.

"Come in one day and found them holding fire to Ollie's hand, trying to make him talk. I run them off right quick and ever since then they been trying to grab Ollie!"

"Looks like they could see that Ollie can't tell them anything."

"They think he's just fooling, making out like he ain't right."

"Harper told us he was going to make him talk, or kill him trying," Aaron said, leaning the now-loaded rifle against the wall. "What he'll have to do, too, because Ollie sure can't talk or nothing—even if he knowed something. Them convicts fixed him up for good."

"This Harper have any proof that you were in on the holdup?"

"Nope, only thinks so because we was sent to the pen for it. They're claiming we both had a hand in it, that after it was over, it was Ollie that had the saddlebag full of gold while the rest of the gang suckered the posse off into the hills. There was a shooting and the others got themselves killed—leaving Ollie with all the money."

"That the way it was?"

Aaron shook his head. "Was nothing like that, nothing to it at all. Ollie and me—we wasn't the ones in on it, but there was a couple of fellows that claimed they'd seen the holdup and they swore we was part of the gang. We went to the pen on their say-so."

"They made a big mistake, them two that said it was Ollie and Aaron," Ma King added, relighting her pipe. "Maybe they looked like my boys but it wasn't them. The law same as said so itself when it turned them loose."

It was possible, Shawn admitted to himself. Errors in identification had been made before by persons who, under the stress of excitement, believed they were seeing someone only to have subsequent facts prove them wrong; and likely it would happen again. . . . Still . . .

"What about the convicts that beat up Ollie while you were in prison? They must have known something."

"They was listening to rumors, that's all," Aaron replied. "Word gets in behind the walls fast sometimes, and part of that bunch who cornered Ollie the day we was all out building road, was due to be turned loose. Their time was up. Reckon they figured to find out from him where he'd hid the gold and go after it themselves soon's they got freed."

"Why didn't they try to find out from you?"

"Was Ollie that had—I'm meaning, that they claimed had it and buried it."

"But if you were with him—"

"Now, hold on!" Ma King broke in, frowning. "Way you're putting it, it's the same as saying Ollie and Aaron was mixed up in it!"

Starbuck brushed back his hat, cocked his head to one side. "Little hard to believe everybody was wrong; the law, the men who identified them, the convicts who wanted to find the money—and now Harper. Expect you've heard of the old saying that where there's a wet place there had to have been some water."

"Don't mean a thing where my boys are concerned. I know them—and they sure wouldn't get all clabbered up in something like that. Ollie's a little wild maybe— or was. I'll nod to that, but he'd never take part in no holdup. Aaron wouldn't either."

"Expect you can tell that from the way I handle a

gun," the elder son said. "Never was no good at it."

"He's the worker of the family," Ma added. "Never had no time for nothing except working the place. Was Ollie that sort of took after his pa—in some ways."

Shawn, aware that Dora still watched him intently, and beginning to feel uncomfortable under the steady pressure of her gaze, glanced through the window to the country beyond. There was no sign of Harper and his outlaw friends. He would like to think they had given up but now, after hearing the reason for their presence, he had small hope.

He came around slowly, thoughtfully. Aaron had crossed to the kitchen area, had found a chunk of cold cornbread and was munching at it hungrily. Dora, at last breaking her engrossment, was moving to where Ollie sat. She halted there, began to fuss with his shirt collar. Ma King, however, had not turned away. Pipe jutting from her mouth, she met his glance head-on, a faint aura of defiance still clinging to her.

"This holdup, where'd it take place?"

"Colorado," Aaron said before his mother could make a reply. "Town called Enterprise."

"You there when it happened?"

"Sure was," King answered, and then glancing at his mother, checked his words. "Was there on business," he finished lamely.

Starbuck's shoulders lifted, fell. He wasn't getting all of the story; he was convinced of that now. But the need to know the truth was important. Their lives could depend on it.

"Think you folks had better face up to something," he said. "Harper's going to hit us again. I'm pretty sure of that, and this time there's a good chance we won't be able to stop him. Your ammunition's not going to hold out—for one thing.

"On top of that they're holding all the good cards. There's fire, for one thing. They can pin us down inside while they put a torch to the place."

Shawn hesitated, allowed his words to sink in. Then, "I figure our best chance lies in trying to talk to them, make them understand it wasn't Ollie and Aaron in that robbery—that it was somebody else."

Aaron tossed the remaining bit of cornbread into the wood box, settled back against the table. Ma King removed the corncob from her mouth, stared fixedly at the bowl.

"Ain't no use trying," she said. "Chet Harper won't listen."

"Why? He got a good reason?"

The old woman took the pipe by the stem, knocked the bowl against the heel of her hand to loosen the dottle. "Just won't, that's why."

Aaron heaved a deep sigh, crossed to her side. "He's guessing, Ma, and he's coming close. I reckon he's entitled to the truth—helping us like he's done."

Ma King stared at the blackened tobacco lying on the floor at her feet. Finally she nodded, raised her lined face to Shawn.

"Aaron's right. We wasn't exactly telling you the truth—all of it, anyway."

12 ~~~

Ollie King stirred irritably, made a small, childish sound. Dora turned at once to the water bucket, and ladling out a quantity in the tin dipper that hung above, carried it to the man. Ma King watched, her expression unchanging as he clawed at the container, sloshed a part of its contents down his shirt front in his eagerness to consume it.

"You ain't some kind of a lawman are you?" she asked, finally.

Starbuck said, "No."

The woman's shoulders settled forward, and with a slight motion of her head, she started toward the kitchen area. In that moment a great weariness seemed to come over her and the tough bravado she affected appeared to melt, fall away.

"You tell him, Aaron," she murmured. "Time I was getting some eats together. Like as not supper'll be a long time coming here. . . . Dora, peel up a pan of spuds."

The girl wheeled at once, followed her to the table near the stove and began to help with the preparation. of the past-due noon meal. Aaron, first quenching the thirst the cornbread had kindled, crossed to the front of the room. He pointed to one of the chairs.

"Might as well set."

Shawn waved the offer aside, continued to stand at the window. "Best I keep an eye out for Harper."

Aaron bobbed, sank into the chair himself. "Was sort of a accident, me being there in Enterprise," he said. "Went after Ollie."

"Then he was there?"

"Yeah. Never was much for staying around the place, was always slipping off, going to Santa Fe or Vegas or some other town. Was a fellow that liked to be where things was going on—which there sure ain't around here. Ain't never nothing but a powerful lot of god-awful work that never ends."

"You running any cattle?"

"Nope, sold off what we had. Just got the farming patch, the chickens, and one old cow."

"No horses? How do you do your plowing?"

"Oh, we got a mare. She's old, too, but she does pretty good. Sold Ollie's bay a while back. Was no need keeping him—and we was needing cash. Shame, sure was a fine animal.

"Anyways, I went up there after Ollie. He'd sort of teamed up with a couple other fellows, punchers riding north to Wyoming, where they aimed to take a job on some ranch. They'd first got together over in Elizabeth-town, got all liquored up, and wound up later in Enterprise.

"We didn't know about that and Ma and Dora and me wasn't much worried. Ollie was always doing something like that, riding off and then showing up a couple of days later saying he was sorry and the like. Afterwards he'd settle down, do his share around here for a spell—leastwise 'til the itch got into him again."

"Then you got wind that he was in Enterprise—"

Aaron nodded slowly, seemingly listening to the crackling sound of grease turning hot in a skillet on the stove.

"Was more'n a week later and Ma was getting sort of worried. Me, I was getting mad, all the work piling up—the kind Ma and Dora couldn't do. Fellow rode by, said he'd run into Ollie up there and had a message for us from him. Said to tell us he was all right and he'd be home soon.

"Another week went by and no Ollie. Ma started getting her dander up then and after a couple, three more days, she sent me to get him.

"Found him right off—Enterprise ain't such a big place—but he wasn't ready to come home. Said he had a big deal a-stewing and if it worked out right he'd be ready to come back with enough money in his pocket to fix it so's we could plain forget this here place and get us a ranch that'd amount to something."

"Was like his pa that way," Ma King said, looking over her shoulder. "Always having big ideas and wanting to make things nice for me and the others."

"Big ideas is all it ever was—for both of them," Aaron murmured.

The older woman whirled. "Now, I won't have you bad-mouthing your pa like that! He was a good man, better'n most in some ways, and I won't let you go disrespecting him!"

"Ain't disrespecting him, only speaking what's gospel, Ma, and you know it."

Shawn glanced again to the empty, quiet land beyond the yard. No one lived without trouble, it seemed; everyone had a measure of problems, it was only that some had more than others. He had his—Ben, finding him, and the settling of old Hiram's estate—all of which was being forced into the background while he took a hand in the Kings' affairs.

But he had grown accustomed to such interruptions and delays, for, try as he might, he was continually finding himself involved. He guessed he should care less about others, should turn a deaf ear to their adversities, and permit them to work it out themselves— capable of doing so or not. . . . But he could never ignore anyone who needed help; he hadn't been brought up that way.

"This big deal of Ollie's—was it the holdup?"

Aaron nodded. "Didn't know that right off, but that was it. Him and four other men he'd fell in with while he was laying around a saloon, they got word that a Wells-Fargo bank shipment was coming through. Was to be fifty thousand dollars in gold coin. . . . Totted up to ten thousand apiece, which sure is a lot of money. Well, they pulled off the robbery."

Startled, Shawn came fully around. "You saying now that Ollie was in on it?"

"He was, and it was just like everybody said. He was handed the money and him and some other fellow took off with it while the rest of the gang let the posse chase them off into another direction—"

"And got themselves killed," Ma finished.

80

Ollie King began to whimper softly. Dora paused, picked up a square of cornbread, placed it in his hand. He pressed it against his mouth, began to devour it wolfishly. The girl turned away quickly, resumed her duties at the cook table.

"Next thing I knowed," Aaron continued, "the sheriff come after me and took me off to jail. He had Ollie there, too, only they wouldn't let us see each other. Then a couple of men showed up, looked at me, and said yes, I sure was the one they'd seen ride off with Ollie and them other outlaws after the robbing was over.

"The sheriff started in then trying to make me tell where we'd cached the gold, and I reckoned from that Ollie'd hid it somewheres but since we didn't get to do no talking together, I was in the dark about what he'd told them.

"Wasn't 'til later when we was up before the judge that I found out Ollie was saying no to the whole thing and was claiming he wasn't one of the gang and that he didn't never see no gold."

"You believe him?"

Aaron shifted, scratched at the stubble on his jaw as he fixed his eyes on his brother. "I seen them that got killed and they was the ones he had that there big deal on with."

The cabin was warming from the fire in the stove and beginning to fill with the sizzling noise of frying meat and bacon and the smell of chicory.

"Don't quite savvy you," Starbuck said. "Seems to me you're not for sure he was in on it."

"He ain't," Ma King said.

"I reckon he was," Aaron drawled, quietly stubborn. "Ma just never would believe he could've done it, but I know better. Ollie had that gold, and he hid it somewheres. I figure he thought right up to the time we rode through them gates into the pen that we was going to be turned loose—only we wasn't."

"What about the man who was with him, if it wasn't you?"

"It dang sure wasn't me—and I don't know nothing about him! Ollie told me once he was dead. How it come to be he never did say."

Starbuck struggled to sort out the facts in his head, but he was having trouble. A lot of the pieces didn't seem to fit.

"Didn't Ollie try to clear you, make the judge see that you weren't the one with him?"

"Sure. Done his best, but nobody'd believe him. We was brothers and we'd been seen in the town together. And then them two coming and saying I was the one— we didn't have much chance of proving anything."

"How long were you in the pen before Ollie got hurt?"

"Eight—no was nine months."

"And he never told you what had happened to the gold in all that time?"

"Wouldn't even talk about it. Always put me off, saying the thing for us to do was work hard at what the jailers told us to do and not start no trouble. That way we'd be turned loose in a couple of years or so and we could go back to Ma and Dora and take up living where we'd left off."

"You think he had in mind to then go dig up the gold where he'd buried it?"

Aaron looked down at his hands. "What I would guess."

"But when those convicts caught him, beat him up—"

"They plain put a end to plans like that. Where he hid all that money nobody'll ever know. It's lost, gone for good unless'n somebody just happens to stumble on it."

Ma King had hesitated at her chores again, was studying Aaron from across the room. "All that's nothing but you thinking and guessing," she said. "Ollie never did come right out and tell you he done it."

"No, never did, but I know, Ma, same as down deep, you know. Only wish't he had told me everything so's I could go find that gold and take it back to the Wells-Fargo people and get shed of all the trouble we're having."

"Should be able to make Harper understand," Shawn said. "A man can see that Ollie, whether he did it or not, won't ever be able to tell anybody anything. You said they tried forcing him, found out they couldn't. Can't see why they won't accept it and leave you folks alone."

Aaron King got to his feet. Moving to the door, he opened it and glanced out. "There's something you're forgetting, Starbuck. They think I was the man with Ollie, same as the law did—and they figure I know right where the money's hid."

13 〜〜

He finally had the whole story, Shawn thought. Everything now fit into place—particularly the reason why Chet Harper and his outlaw friends refused to give up and ride on. Failing to get the information they wanted from poor, addled Ollie, they had turned on Aaron.

"The truth helps," he said. "Can see better what we're up against."

Dora, in the act of setting food on the table, glanced up at him. "That mean you'll stay?" she asked, breaking her long silence.

"Changes nothing. Got into this and I'll see it through."

A relieved smile parted her lips. Ma King, bearing a platter of fried potatoes and sliced salt pork, flashed the girl a speculative look and frowned. "Reckon we can eat," she said, depositing the large stoneware plate. "You menfolks come on."

Aaron moved forward obediently. Shawn, making another sweeping survey through the window and seeing no indication of the outlaws, followed. Settling onto a chair, he watched Dora conduct Ollie to his place at the table, fill a plate, and start him eating, her features calm, her manner patient.

It wasn't much of a life for her, he guessed, helping himself to the food profferred by Aaron. Her time appeared to be occupied almost solely by caring for Ollie and tending to his needs.

The meal was eaten in silence. Starbuck, discovering himself hungry, relished the good if simple food, even to the black and bitter chicory coffee. When it was finished, Ma, more the motherly housewife than the hard-bitten, rough-talking old harridan he had encountered in the brush, waved him and Aaron back to the front of the cabin and, with Dora, began to clear the table and clean the kitchen.

Aaron, sinking once again into his chair, watched her with puzzled eyes. It was evident from his concern that she ordinarily didn't trouble herself with such womanly duties but probably left them to the girl; and such a change he found disturbing.

Shawn, giving it brief thought, realized there was a difference, and wondered, too. But it could be attributed to the novelty of having company even under trying circumstances, or it was possible that having another man in the house was triggering a release, one that freed her from the necessity of enacting the role as strong father-figure of the family.

"You going to try and do some talking to Harper?" Aaron asked as Shawn took up his position at the window.

"Costs nothing—and there's always the chance it might do some good."

"Just be wasting your breath," King said, searching his pockets for pipe and tobacco. "Sure do wish Ollie'd told me what he done with that gold. Be glad to tell him just where—"

"Be the wrong thing to do. Not theirs."

"Know that but I'd tell them anyway just to get rid of them, make them leave us be."

Dora had gotten Ollie onto his feet and was coaxing him into the bedroom in the corner of the cabin, where he could lie down and be out of the way if trouble returned. Ma King had finished her chores, was drying her hands on the apron she had restored to her waist.

"Expect that'd be the only thing that will make them pull out. They're going to believe what they want to."

Aaron, his pipe going, leaned back. "Expect you've seen a-plenty of their kind before."

"My share. World's full of Harpers—and they're all pretty much alike."

"Reminds me, when you first showed up you said something about bringing us word from somebody—"

"Man named Cameron in Cimarron. Wanted you to know about Hillister."

"Who's he?"

"Bounty hunter. Got it in his head that he has to lay every outlaw in the country by the heels and haul them into the law, dead or alive—doesn't make any differ-ence to him."

"What's he want with us?"

"Thinks you and Ollie ought to be back in the pen."

"But the judge—and the Governor, they—"

"Your getting pardoned doesn't mean a thing to him. Still outlaws to his way of looking at it and he's loco enough to try and put you there again."

Aaron shrugged. "Once he sees Ollie and it's all explained to him, he'll maybe forget it."

"Not Hillister. Man can't be reasoned with. Catching outlaws is like a crusade with him—and he's dangerous. As soon kill as not."

"Sounds like you had some truck with him."

"Did—and I was lucky. Managed to talk hard enough to keep myself alive until we could get to the sheriff in Cimarron. He made Hillister turn me loose but that didn't end it. Tried to ambush me on the way here but I got by him. He'll still be hunting me."

Aaron frowned. "Why? If the sheriff told him you wasn't wanted, why's he still after you?"

"Wouldn't believe what he was told. Says I look like an outlaw because of the way I wear my gun—and that's enough for him. It'll be the same with you and Ollie. You've been branded and far as he's concerned that means you either ought to be behind bars—or dead."

King came forward in his chair. "You telling me that he'll try taking us back to the pen, or maybe even kill us if he has to?"

"Exactly what you can figure on. That's the reason I stopped by here. Wanted to warn you about him."

Shawn became aware that Ma and Dora were standing quietly by, listening. The older woman, hands clasped under her apron, moved deeper into the room.

"Where's this Hillister now?"

Shawn nodded toward the window, at the country now beginning to soften as the afternoon wore on.

"Out there, somewhere. Probably hunted me for a time, then gave up and started looking for your place."

"Meaning he don't know where we live?"

"He'll find it. . . . I did."

Aaron shifted wearily. "Then we got him to worry about on top of Harper and his bunch," he said in a ragged tone.

Ma King crossed to him, laid a hand on his shoulder. "Don't fret, son. We can take care of him same as we can Chet Harper." Turning, she faced Starbuck. "Seems I'm beholden to you again—and I'm obliged. Not many folks would've bothered."

"Mad dog running loose is everybody's business."

Ma's lined features softened as a partial smile came to her lips. "Reckon your pa and ma can be real proud of you. They live around here somewheres?"

"Both dead. We had a farm in Ohio."

"And after they was gone you picked up and come west."

"Not just that way—came to find my brother. I've been hunting him for quite a time. On my way to Santa Fe now."

"He waiting there for you?"

"Could be. Don't know for sure. I've gone to a lot of places thinking he might be, but it's turned out I was wrong."

"Well, I'm sorry if we've caused you to maybe miss out on him. . . . Must be sort of lonesome-like traipsing around all over the country like you're doing."

"Used to it now—and someday it'll end. I'll find him."

"Expect you will all right," the older woman said in

a gentle tone. "I'm hoping it'll be soon. Be a shame was you to waste your years and end up being old with no life left to live. Man like you ought to have a home—a family."

"Someday," Starbuck said, glancing through the window. "Aim to do—"

He drew up sharply, whatever he intended saying dying on his lips. Riders had appeared in the brush beyond the cleared ground.

"They're here," he said.

14 ~~~

Fear tore at Aaron King. Without conscious thought he came out of his chair in a quick lunge. Snatching up the rifle, he crowded close to the window.

From the corner of his eye he saw Ma shrug resignedly, and, disregarding the belted gun under her apron, take possession of the shotgun Dora had used and cross to Starbuck's side.

"They coming or waiting?" he heard her ask.

"Waiting," Starbuck said.

He saw her look past the tall man's shoulder into the yard. "That big one on the brown horse—he's Chet Harper. 'Pears he's lost somebody. . . . Tex, I reckon it is."

"He's the one Starbuck winged," Aaron volunteered.

Ma made no comment. After a moment he saw her step back. "What're you wanting us to do?" she asked, looking straight at Starbuck.

"Let them make the first move. It's their game; we'll call when the right time comes."

Aaron watched Ma turn to him, heard her sharp voice. "You got that straight? Don't do nothing until Starbuck tells you to."

In the quiet that filled the cabin he stared at his parent. Disbelief was running through him. To have her defer to another was a new and extraordinary experience. Always, about as far back as he could recall, hers was the word, the law, the final, irrevocable decision.

"All right, Ma," he murmured.

Doubt was threading his voice but the years of subservience to her will were having their effect; if she wanted to let Starbuck handle things, he reckoned she knew what she was doing. Maybe it was best, anyway. Starbuck was a cool customer. He'd been around, likely had seen a lot of trouble. He'd know how to stand up to Chet Harper.

He wished he could be like the tall, hard-jawed rider. It would have pleased Pa. He'd wanted a man such as Starbuck for a son, instead he'd got Ollie and he'd got him—a slough-footed plodder who could barely ride a horse and was even worse when it came to handling a gun.

His place was in the fields. Pa'd told him that a long time ago, and he'd known the words were true. And with the same practical logic, he'd made the best of it, not minding too much when Ollie'd go tearing off for a hell raising in some town and leave everything for him to do.

When Pa died and Ma had stepped right into his boots, which she'd more or less been doing all along, he still hadn't thought much about it. Actually, he realized one day, he should have taken over as head of the family, being the elder son; but Ma hadn't given him the chance, had simply gathered up the reins herself and took charge.

He supposed it was right. He wasn't the strong kind, the sort who could be boss and get things done by ordering others around. And he was no hand to argue and fight; way he saw it, when there was something to be done, the thing to do was do it—not talk about it. It was easier than yammering and fussing and being responsible.

Aaron guessed that was the heart of it: he just didn't have it in him to accept responsibilities—except where chores around the place were concerned. He could do that and he'd been doing it just about all of the thirty years he'd been alive, but as long as he was being honest with himself he might as well own up to the fact that he wasn't even much good at doing that. While Pa was alive, they did have a ranch of sorts—a few head of cattle, a good stand of hay, a few hogs, horses and such, along with the prospects of doing better.

But after Pa died, things went down fast despite all he could do; it was like stepping onto a mudbank along the river—you started sliding and you couldn't stop no mater how hard you tried. Maybe it was his fault the place had turned into a starved-out, sod-buster's patch; maybe he should have set Ma down and taken over the way an older son was supposed to do.

Aaron shrugged as he stared morosely at the low hills beyond the yard. He could just see himself ordering Ma around, making Ollie toe the mark, and such. They would've laughed in his face. But it might've worked out. If Ma hadn't right away jumped in and made herself the boss, he would have been forced to assume the job as head of the family, and having responsibility thrust onto him, he maybe would have come into his own and amounted to something.

One thing sure, if that had panned out, he bet Dora wouldn't look at him the way she did; in fact, she probably wouldn't even be there with them—and he wasn't certain he liked that thought.

Stirring, Aaron glanced to where Ma and Starbuck were standing at the window, their attention on Harper and his men. An ease settled over him. There was no denying it was a relief to have someone like them doing all the thinking, saying what was to be done. . . . Still, if he had the chance to live it all over again and had his druthers, he'd like to at least try being his own man—be one who did the telling and not just the listening.

Dora seated herself on one of the chairs in the kitchen and settled her eyes on Ma and the stranger. The dishes and pans were all cleaned and put away and there was nothing to do now but sit and wait—and look after Ollie.

That was the routine her life followed—cooking,

cleaning, housekeeping such as it was, and taking care of Ollie. It was not the life she had envisioned, and certainly not one she would have let herself in for had she known. Now, like a rabbit caught in a web snare, she was trapped, unable to escape into a world bright with promise because of circumstance.

It had been different in the beginning. Orphaned at seventeen, she had made the long journey from the plains of Illinois to Santa Fe, where she was to live with her only remaining relatives, a childless aunt and uncle who owned and operated a small store in the ancient Spanish and Mexican capital. To pay for her keep she had gone to work at once in the establishment.

On the second day she was there, Ollie King had ridden into town with several friends, and subsequently dropped into the store, alone, to make a purchase. He had stopped short when he saw her and from that moment on could not take his eyes off her.

He finally did leave, only to return that same evening, and under the disapproving glances of her uncle, told her straight out that she was the prettiest thing he'd ever seen, that he was in love with her and never again would he be worth a hoot unless she married him.

He was a redheaded, reckless, laughing man not much older than she and said that he lived with his mother and brother on a ranch east of the mountains. It wasn't much of a place, he admitted frankly, but it had good prospects and with her to fire him up he knew he could turn it into a real home and a moneymaker.

On the fourth day she succumbed to his proposal, agreeing also to wait until they got to the ranch before going through the marriage ceremony. They could have it performed in Cimarron, a town they were fairly near, and he wanted very much to have his mother and brother in attendance. It shouldn't matter to her, he'd said, for after all, she had no close family to think about; the aunt and uncle, who washed their hands of the whole affair from the start, didn't count.

It took days for the shock of what she had come into to wear off: a pipe-smoking, hard-swearing old woman with a will of iron who made it plain that she hated every inch of her because she had hooked her son; a spineless brother who slunk about, tight-lipped, doing chores on a place so hardscrabble poor that it was below the level of even the worst tenant farm.

The wedding was out of the question for the time being; Ma King made that clear within minutes after they arrived and Ollie had announced their plans. There was too much work to be done. Things were way behind, thanks to Ollie's being gone, which, Dora gathered from listening to them talk, was an unpredictable frailty of his. Once they were caught up they'd all go to Cimarron and let the Baptist preacher get the job done.

Meanwhile, everything was to be kept decent, Ma declared, and had her two sons clean out the small shack at one end of the yard and fix it up as living quarters for Dora. After the marriage was performed, Ollie could move in.

It was all a terrible letdown for her, but she had made her bargain and there was no going back to Santa Fe and her aunt and uncle or, because of the isolation, to anywhere else. And so she fell into the servile system under which Ollie and his brother, Aaron, existed, soon impassively accepting the acid-tongued comments, directives, and rebukes of Ma King while she awaited the day when they would all make the trip to Cimarron, after which she and Ollie could at least live together.

But that never came to pass. Ollie, goaded by the old restlessness, mounted his horse one night when everyone was asleep and rode north—into trouble, and she never again saw the man as she had known him. He did write her a letter just before he was taken off to the pen and for that she would always be grateful.

While Ollie and Aaron were away serving their time, she stayed on with Ma partly because there was no other place to go, but mostly because of Ollie and the future they could have together if ever given the chance. And then when the pardons came through and he was back alive but, for all purposes, dead, she found herself facing the fact that if she was to have the life she now dreamed of, she must break away, find it for herself.

This hope was now stirring with greater vigor within her, brought to a shining glow by the man who had ridden into their midst with the thought in mind to warn Ma and Aaron of a threat, but who stayed on to lend them a hand.

Starbuck—tall, dark, cool-eyed, and steady-nerved,

represented all that Ollie had not been: strength, courage, dependability, and with a knowledge of the world outside the tiny circle that imprisoned her—he could give her all that. And now as she sat watching him, the determination not to miss the opportunity began to crystallize.

She would offer him herself—everything, asking only that he take her with him when he rode out. If taking a wife was not in the scheme of things for him, then she would be his woman, hoping that love would finally come and grow and become a part of their relationship.

Failing that persuasion she would ask only that he enable her to reach the nearest town of any size, one where she could strike out on her own. The important thing was that she leave, that she put Ollie and Ma and grubbing, hungering Aaron with their starved-out cabbage patch behind her before it was too late.

But it would all have to wait until matters with Chet Harper were settled—and that would come to pass. Starbuck was a man—the kind who could handle anything.

15 ~~~

"Just can't keep on calling you Starbuck," Ma King said, continuing to look through the window at the riders in the brush beyond the yard. "You got another name?"

"Shawn."

"Sounds Indian. There some Indian blood in you?"

"No. My mother was a schoolteacher. Once taught some kids from the Shawnee tribe. Liked the sound of the word, I reckon, and when I came along she made it into a name for me."

"Kind of pretty at that," the older woman said. "What do you figure Harper's up to?"

At that moment one of the outlaws pulled away from the others, angled toward a high mound of rock and brush at the edge of the clearing.

"Looks like we're about to find out," Starbuck replied.

"Harper's coming," Aaron announced unnecessarily from the opposite end of the wall.

"Let him. Probably wants to talk."

The outlaw rode in behind the buttelike rise, dismounted, taking care to not make a target of himself. Moving to the edge of the rocks that fronted on the cabin, he removed his hat, waved it overhead.

"You Kings there in the house—you listening?"

Shawn stepped to the door, opened it slightly. "We hear you!" he yelled back.

"Aiming to give you a last chance. Tell me where that gold's hid and we'll pull out, let you be."

"Can't tell you because we don't know."

Silence followed for a brief time and then Harper's voice came again. "That you talking, Aaron?"

"No. Friend of the family. Name's Starbuck."

"It's him I want to talk to. You keep out of this, mister."

"Aaron ain't got nothing to say," Ma shouted through

the broken window. "Starbuck's doing the talking for us."

"You best forget the whole thing," Shawn added. "Aaron doesn't know where the gold is. Never did. He wasn't in on the holdup."

"Know better. He was there, all right."

"You just think so, like a lot of other folks did. Was somebody else with Ollie. Could be he looked like Aaron, but it wasn't him."

Once more there was quiet. Down in the field below the garden a meadowlark whistled cheerfully.

"How come you've stuck your snout in this, Starbuck?" the outlaw called finally. "You fixing it so's you can get that gold for yourself?"

"Told you—just a friend—"

"The hell!" Harper shouted scornfully. "You're after it same as me."

"If I was I wouldn't be hanging around here trying to find it. Get this in your head, Harper—Aaron doesn't know where that money is—only Ollie does, and you've seen the shape he's in. The gold's lost, cached somewhere, and it'll stay there until somebody stumbles onto it, turns it up—"

"That's a lot of bull!"

"It's the straight truth, and you better make up your mind to it and pull out. Any shooting or killing won't change anything—so forget it."

"Ain't about to, mister—"

"You pay attention to him, Chet Harper!" Ma shouted. "He's telling you the gospel truth!"

"And I'm telling you, old woman—I'm giving you one hour to send Aaron out here ready to talk! You don't, then we're coming after him."

"Done tried that a couple a times, ain't you? All it got you was some bullets. Be the same again."

"Maybe not. I figure a little fire'll do more good than bullets."

Ma King drew back, nodded to Shawn. "That's what you said he'd try—but I just never believed it. Is he just talking or do you think he'll do it?"

"Expect he will."

The old woman turned away, glanced around the cabin. "Sure would hate that," she murmured. "It ain't much but me and Cain built it ourselves—and it's all I got."

Cain . . . Cain King . . . He would have been her husband, Shawn guessed. Anger stirring through him suddenly, he swung back to the partly open door.

"Why don't you leave these folks alone, Harper? They can't tell you where that gold is—none of them!"

"Know better—"

"You don't know anything—you're just thinking they can—and I'll give you a bit of warning; you try burning down this place and there'll be some men die —you first of all if I can manage it!"

He knew he was probably wasting breath, that his words would have little effect on what the outlaws would eventually attempt. The odds were all against the Kings, and him, cooped up in the cabin as they were. Chet Harper had only to keep them occupied with part of his gang while he sent others to set fires that would quickly consume the cabin.

"Could be," the outlaw said, "there won't be no need for none of that—not if you show some sense. What say if I make you a deal?"

"Doubt if anything you come up with will interest the Kings."

"Ought to, spot they're in. . . . I look at it this way; there's enough gold there for all of us. You tell Aaron to take me to where they buried it and after we dig it up I'll hand over five thousand dollars of it to him. . . . Five thousand—that's a lot of money!"

"No doubt, but it comes right back to the same thing—Aaron doesn't know where it's buried—"

"And if he did, I sure wouldn't let him do it!" Ma shouted. "Why, I wouldn't trust you, Chet Harper, no farther'n I could throw a Missouri mule by the tail!"

"Better do some thinking on it, old woman."

"Ain't no need—"

"With all that much gold you could turn this dump into a mighty nice little farm—even get yourself a few head of cattle and start living like white folks—"

"Go to hell, goddamn you!" Ma King exploded suddenly, once again her old self. "I ain't listening, so you might as well quit the yammering."

"What about you, Starbuck?" Harper said then, calmly ignoring the woman's words. "You willing to make a deal?"

"My answer's the same as Ma's, and if you try pushing us, you're going to get some of your bunch killed."

"Not the way I see it, and I expect you'll be changing your mind after you've set on it a bit."

"Not likely."

"Just wait and see. . . . Now, I'll be back in a hour. You have Aaron ready to talk, or travel. Don't make no difference to me which. I figure I'm being good to you, offering to give you some of the gold like I am. But if you've still got your neck bowed, then we'll get him the hard way. I making myself plain?"

"Reckon you are!" Ma shouted. "Now, I'll make something plain to you—if you come back, come ready to die!"

16 ~~~

Starbuck wheeled, crossed to the back of the cabin. There was one small window high in the wall beyond the cookstove, and a plank door similar to the front entrance. Opening it quickly, he glanced around, swore softly.

Harper was smart. While he talked, two of his riders had moved into position. There was now one on either side of the house, sitting their horses well back in the brush, where they could effectively keep watch over the cabin and prevent anyone from leaving by the rear while still maintaining a surveillance of the front.

Reaching the barn or any of the structures adjacent to it was out of the question; the yard had been cleared of all brush of any size and a man endeavoring to cross would be at the mercy of the outlaws' guns. He could forget his thoughts of stationing himself in one of the outside buildings and being where he could set up a sort of crossfire should the situation deteriorate into a shootout—which appeared very likely.

It would be possible to slip through the doorway and, by keeping in the ragged shrubbery, make his way to the areas on either side of the cabin where the two outlaws were waiting, but there would be little gained by that. He might be able to disable one before the others became aware of his presence, and that small reduction of the odds hardly seemed worth the risk.

Shawn drew back, frowned, noting as he did that his sorrel, abandoned earlier when Ma King had taken him captive, was standing at the water trough near the well. The big horse had evidently tired of waiting and moved on of its own accord. It had halted, however, in an unsafe place, one where it would be in line with bullets fired at the house that went astray. But there was nothing he could do about it—only hope that the gelding, after taking its fill of water, would wander on into the barn in search of food.

Starbuck continued to stand in the opening, getting the lay of the land firmly established in his mind, and then reentered the room, closing the door and dropping the bar into place.

He did not mention the two outlaws on sentry duty, seeing no point in further alarming the Kings, but simply crossed over to the front and resumed his stand at the window. Harper and the remaining outlaws were no longer visible in the tall growth beyond the yard, but that they were there was a certainty.

He turned about once more, allowed his eyes to sweep the interior of the cabin. It had but the two doors and three windows—possibly a fourth if there was one in the partitioned-off square that made up a bedroom. It didn't matter; all were small and would not permit the passage of a man through them, being designed primarily for the admittance of light and air.

The place was much like a fort, and there was little doubt in Starbuck's mind that against bullets they could more than hold their own. Fire was a different matter; should Harper make good his threat to put a torch to the cabin, they could offer little if any defense.

He glanced around at Ma and Aaron King, at Dora. Each was silent, occupied at the moment with private thoughts. He wondered if they realized the seriousness of their predicament—decided they did but were spending no time in the consideration.

They were people accustomed to crisis, to facing calamity in all its various forms, be it an act of nature or man instigated. Disaster, danger, and utter failure were not strangers to them. In stoical silence they had weathered the howling, cruel winters, the scorching, drought-ridden summers, the onslaughts of disease— even man's hard-handed punishment for wrongdoing.

Now the object of persecution—this time by the enemies of the selfsame law that had scored them in the past—they were accepting the offense with stolid resignation, seemingly reassured by the knowledge that they had survived before and would do so again.

Starbuck was finding it difficult to share their confidence. In an out-and-out battle with guns he would have few qualms; forted up such as they were they could give a good accounting of themselves even with restricted stores of ammunition. But fire—he shook his head, fully aware of their helplessness should the cabin be put to the torch. They would be pinned down, caught in a trap from which escape would be at the whim of outlaws guarding the doors with ready pistols.

"You think we ought to be getting ourselves set?" Aaron asked in a low voice.

"Not much we can do now but wait," Starbuck replied grimly.

17 ~~~

Ma paused at the doorway leading into the bedroom that had been hers and Cain's but now was only a lonely tomb of memories in which she spent the nights. Ollie, his mouth blared open, his body slack, looked like nothing more than a skin sack of bones. He had been a handsome boy, laughing and reckless and much the same as Cain, but wildness had brought an end to all that.

Turning, she glanced to where Starbuck and Aaron, coffeecups in hand, were sitting. Aaron was nervous—it was easy to see that—but Starbuck, his wide shoulders relaxed, his strong features composed, might have been a man with his mind occupied with nothing more than thoughts of his next meal. He was one to lean on, have deep feelings about—there was no denying that. Little wonder Dora couldn't keep her eyes off him.

Dora . . . Ma looked down at the empty cup she held, crossed slowly to the stove to where coffee simmered in its pot. Taking up the chipped, granite container, she refilled her cup and settled down at the table opposite the girl.

"He reminds me of my Cain," she said quietly.

Startled, Dora's eyes spread. "What—"

"Starbuck. Said he reminded me of my mister, some. You're a-wishing you could go off with him."

The girl stared at the older woman for a long breath, then nodded. "Guess I do, Ma. Maybe it's wrong, but I can't help feeling that way."

Ma King slid a glance over her shoulder at the two men. They were beyond overhearing.

"You come here to be Ollie's wife," she said.

"I know that—and I wanted to be, only it just never did happen. And now, coming back from the pen the way he is—there's no use, no sense in it."

"Reckon I understand."

Dora leaned forward, her features tense. "Do you, Ma? Oh, I hope so! There's nothing left for me here, no reason to keep on staying. I'd be wasting my life."

"What about Aaron?"

The girl frowned. "Aaron? I—I—"

"He's wanting you, too, maybe more'n Ollie ever did. He ain't much, God knows, but he's sure and he's steady."

"I never thought of him. Oh, I've caught him looking

at me, sometimes trying to help, but I figured he was only being sorry for me."

"It's more'n that."

"But I don't love him, Ma—and I don't think I can stand it here any longer. I have to get away, find a different kind of life, one that's better. Maybe, if Ollie hadn't ended up the way he did and we'd gotten married, I wouldn't be feeling like I do."

"That you've got to get yourself a man?"

"Not so much that—it's that I want to go away, go where there are lots of people, do things, have things —see the big towns."

"All that ain't much good unless you've got yourself a man, too. Happiness comes when there's sharing. Don't amount to nothing if you're alone."

"I know, and I'm hoping Starbuck—"

Ma King raised her eyes to the window above the stove, a softness filling them as she studied the clean blue of the sky beyond.

"It's all right, girl. Ollie's my son but I'm a woman and I know what a woman needs—a strong man who'll make her feel like a woman, let her see that she's wanted. You're missing all that and I can't fault you none for fretting over it.

"Cain was that kind—big and quiet and full of strength and with a way about him that plain told you he could stand up to anything that come along. Just knowing he was around sort of made things all right.

"Nevermind he was a mite on the hard-living, hard-drinking side. He made me know I was his and no other man'd better even look slanchwise at me, else he'd break him in two. And when he roughed me up some getting his way with me, I knowed it was because he loved me. . . . There was a powerful lot of caring in his wanting."

Dora was staring at the older woman in amazement. This was a side of Ma she had not realized existed.

"You must have loved him a terrible lot."

"Reckon I did at that—maybe more'n any woman ought to love a man because it makes the hurt all the worse when the losing time comes. But I always figure we was going to live only once and it was smart to smell the roses while you had the chance. Life ain't never easy, especially for a woman, anyway—slaving and drudging to keep body and soul together, having young'uns and worrying about them while all the time you're holding onto your man, keeping him happy and a-needing you.

"But trying hard as you can it don't always last and when you lose your man something goes out inside you, like maybe somebody turned down the lamp. Things ain't never the same after that. Me, I had to step in take Cain's place, be him and me both. Aaron didn't have the gumption to take over and Ollie just plain didn't give a hoot. All he wanted to do was chase around, raise hell, have hisself a good time.

"Was right pleased when he showed up here with you, telling me you was going to be his wife. Maybe I didn't show it but it pleasured me just the same. Figured maybe he'd changed and was going to settle down, amount to something, but then he went and got all messed up in that robbery and spoilt everything."

Ma King paused, brushed at the sweat on her forehead. The low fire in the stove was making it warm in the cabin, but it was growing late and evening coolness would soon set in, bring relief.

"Expect I oughtn't to be talking to you this here way, me being Ollie's ma, but he ruint his life and there ain't no call to let him ruin yours. I'm seeing what's burning inside you, and like I said, I can't hold it against you."

"Then you'd understand if I went away with Starbuck?"

"Ain't saying I'd be real happy but I know what's chawing away at you. You've got the right to a decent life, which you ain't never going to have here with Ollie. Expect, was I in your shoes, I'd be thinking the same. . . . You sure Starbuck'll take you?"

Dora shook her head. "Aim to talk to him—ask."

"Well, he'll treat you good. Know that from just talking to him, but he won't marry you. Not ready yet. Got his mind set on finding this brother of his and he ain't got time for nothing else until he does. Like Cain that way—points his nose toward something and he won't quit 'til he's there."

"That's all right with me. Never had a man stir me like he does—even Ollie—but if he doesn't feel the same about me then I'll have to settle for just going with him."

"Like a camp follower, that it?"

"Maybe, but mostly so's I can get to a town."

"So's you can find work?"

The girl nodded, her calm face expressionless.

Ma shrugged. "Jobs ain't plentiful in this country for a woman—the decent kind."

"I'll make out."

"Expect you will—and you'll find yourself a man, too. With a little fixing up you can be right pretty."

"I'm glad you don't mind, Ma. I owe you a lot."

"Reckon you've paid your fare and you're entitled. Had my time. Wasn't long as I'd've like for it to be but it was what the good Lord laid out for me, I guess."

"I hate to leave you with Ollie—all that extra work—"

"We'll make out—Aaron and me. When this day's over and all the trouble's been settled, we'll just pick up where we left off, go right on living."

"Thank you, Ma," Dora said. "It means a lot to me."

"Know that. When are you doing your talking to Starbuck?"

"First chance I get."

"Want me to say something to him?"

"No, best I do it myself."

The older woman smiled. If she figured Shawn Starbuck correctly, he'd come to her and find out if she were agreeable to the girl's leaving, anyway. He'd not do anything behind her back.

"Be smart was you to wait until this ruckus is over," she said. "He's got his mind set on it now and he won't take kindly to having his thinking fogged up."

Dora frowned. "I'd like to know—get it settled."

Ma glanced again to the window. "Won't be long. Harper's hour is about gone."

18 ~~~

Shawn held the empty cup in his hands, considered it moodily. He had drained the last of the bitter chicory from it, was flinching from its harsh taste. Across the room Ma and Dora were engaged in low-pitched conversation while in the chair an arm's length from him Aaron sat in frozen silence.

From the bedroom in the corner came the sound of Ollie's measured snoring. He, at least, was out of it, had no worries. Whether they survived the day or not was immaterial to him, for his was a vague and shadowy world in which nothing mattered.

Restless, Shawn rose, stepped to the window. Still no sign of Harper but he guessed the outlaw would be making an appearance soon; the hour's slow, dragging minutes had about run their course. Wheeling, he settled again in his chair, this time facing Aaron King directly.

"Time's about up."

Aaron nodded, glanced at the nearby bench upon which had been piled all of the ammunition they had been able to muster. Beyond it the shotgun and two rifles leaned against the wall.

"Expect we can hold out for a while."

"Could be it won't be necessary—not with Harper talking fire."

"Keg of water there in the kitchen, and the bucket's most near full."

"The blaze will start on the outside. Be no chance to get out and fight it—Harper's already got two men watching from the brush, making sure none of us leaves the cabin."

Aaron's lips tightened. He frowned, stared at the floor.

"You sure you know what's shaping up?"

King bobbed his head. "Course I do."

"There'll be some dying before it's done with. Man ought to keep that from happening, if he could."

Aaron straightened angrily. "You saying I'm lying about that money—that I know where it's hid?"

"Not saying it—"

"Well, it's what you mean."

Starbuck shrugged. "Not just us two in this. We've got Ma and Dora to think about."

"I wasn't lying," King said doggedly. "Told the truth."

"Fair enough. Just wanted you to realize that it could cost us—all of us—our lives. . . . Don't mind losing mine so much if it's for a good reason, but throwing it away for a lie is something else."

"Was I knowing where Ollie hid that gold, I'd tell. Don't want to die any more'n the next man—and I sure wouldn't let Ma and Dora in for it if I could change things somehow. What's set you to thinking I was lying?"

"Harper. Seems plenty sure of what he's doing. All the talking we've done hasn't backed him off a bit."

"He's wrong—and I don't take kindly to be called a liar."

"Don't let it rile you. If you are, you'll likely end up

dead as the rest of us. Be a cinch for them. They get this place to burning, all they have to do is sit back and pick us off when we come out."

"They kill me I sure wouldn't be able to tell them nothing—even if I knew."

"Probably won't kill you right off. Shoot your legs out from under you, maybe break your arms. They'll keep you alive long enough to get what they want."

Shawn was watching Aaron King closely from shuttered eyes. In his own mind he felt the man had been truthful, but Harper's stubborn persistence puzzled him. By this time most men would have concluded they were tracking the wrong bear and turned away; Chet Harper, however, was refusing to admit he was wrong. It was as if he actually knew the Kings were lying about the gold cache.

"You think maybe it'd help was I to go out there and lie to Harper, make out like I was willing to talk and then send him off to the first place I can think of?"

"Might work but only for a bit. Quick as he found out you'd lied it would go worse for all of you."

"Then what's the answer?"

"Already been given. Got to make a stand against him—only way we'll ever satisfy him."

Starbuck paused, shook his head. "Be the same even if you knew where the gold was. It's not Harper's and he has no right to it."

A load seemed to slip from Aaron's shoulders. "Then you're believing me when I tell you I don't know where Ollie hid it?"

"I believe this—that you wouldn't let Ma and Dora in for what's coming if you could stop it."

"Can bet I wouldn't! And I ain't in that big of a hurry to die myself. . . . Don't seem to be bothering you much, though."

"It does—just not showing, maybe. Lot of things I wanted to do before I cash in—got to do, in fact. Big reason why I'm not giving up yet."

"Don't see as we've got much chance, and way you've been talking, you don't think so either."

"Odds are plenty wrong, I'll admit that."

"Then what's making you think it ain't hopeless?"

"Long as we're breathing, we aren't beat. And this cabin's like a fort plenty safe. Bullets can't get through these walls."

"But fire—"

"Thing we've got to do is keep Harper and the others backed off, not let them get near enough to get a blaze started while at the same time we'll be trying to pick them off."

"Can keep that up for a spell, but we ain't got bullets enough to last long."

"I realize that, but we'll take things a jump at a time. Could be something'll turn up that will change the picture. . . . Ma as good with her pistol as she makes out?"

"Plenty—and a lot better'n me."

"How about Dora?"

"Only fair. Knows how to shoot the shotgun and can use a rifle, but she ain't no crack shot."

"If she can aim, pull a trigger, and reload, she'll do.

We'll put her at the back door, tell her if she sees any-thing move, to shoot at it."

"You want me at the end window, same as I was?"

"Good a place as any. I figure most of what'll go on will be out in the front—about the only way they can get at us. I'll take the door, leave the other window for Ma."

Aaron nodded. "Guess Pa knew what he was doing when he didn't cut windows in all the walls. Must've planned on there being times like this."

"Expect so. You remember him?"

"Some. Died when I was ten, or maybe it was eleven years old. Was a big man, did a lot of laughing and whiskey drinking."

"What happened to him?"

"There was an accident. He'd gone hunting for deer. Things was plenty bad and there wasn't much to eat—we was having a hard winter, worst that had come along since the fifties, I heard it said. He took his rifle and went back up on the ridge, about five miles west of here. Don't know for sure what went on but he got a deer and was toting it in.

"Somewhere he must've fell or maybe just dropped the rifle, because he was shot in the belly. He come on in anyway, lugging that big buck so's we'd have meat for the table. . . . Ma done all she could for him, but he'd shed too much blood. Died that next morning."

"Must've been quite a man," Shawn said quietly.

"Yeh, reckon he was. Everything he ever done was for Ma, though. Me and Ollie, we didn't count for much; we was just no more'n a couple of the animals that run around the place. When them two were together it was like there wasn't nobody else alive in the world—only them."

Starbuck made no comment. The attachment between his own parents had been much the same, a strange, powerful bond uniting two dissimilar persons, but they had found room to include both Ben and him in their universe. He shook his head thoughtfully. Being shut out, as had been Aaron and Ollie King, would be terrible.

"Aaron—you coming out?"

Shawn came to his feet quickly, touching the others in the cabin with his glance. "Reckon this is it," he murmured, and turned to the window.

19 ~~~

"Aaron King—you hear me?"

The deadening tension of waiting was over; now began the breathless tension of action. Starbuck looked into the yard. Again, Harper was behind the rocky mound. Two riders were visible beyond him—and there was the pair stationed at the sides of the house. . . . Five in all, counting Harper himself. The man wounded earlier was apparently out of it.

Twisting about, he glanced at Aaron. He was crowded up close to the window, features stiff, a whiteness around his mouth.

"Answer him—"

King started, swallowed hard. "Yeh, I hear you," he shouted.

"You ready to do some talking?"

Aaron turned questioningly to Shawn. Starbuck nodded. "Stall him—keep him busy for a bit while I do some looking around."

King resumed his position. "Ain't nothing I can tell you."

"Hell there ain't!" Harper's retort floated back.

Shawn drew up close to the square of shattered glass, threw his glance out beyond the end of the house. He could not see the outlaw. Frowning, he moved to the opposite side of the sash, probed the area on that, the north part of the yard. There was no one to be seen there either. He gave that thought. Had Harper changed his plans, or had the two outlaws moved in nearer? Could they at that very moment be starting their fires?

". . . Told you I don't know where that gold's hid. Was Ollie that done it, not me."

With Aaron's words beating in his ears, Starbuck wheeled, started for the rear of the cabin. Ma King, rifle in her veined hands, stood beside the kitchen table seemingly awaiting his orders. Dora was nearby. He paused, bucked his head at the older woman.

"Get to the window—keep an eye on that pair in the brush."

Ma, lips compressed, immediately moved to the front of the cabin. Shawn snatched up the shotgun, and holding it by the barrel, passed it to the girl.

"Want you back here," he said, and stepped to the back door.

Dora followed him closely. "Keep to the side," he cautioned, and hunching low, opened the thick panel slowly.

On hands and knees, Starbuck worked his way out onto the narrow stoop to where he could see the brushy flats to either side. A sigh of relief escaped his lips. The outlaws had moved in closer—but only a short distance. Evidently, if such was to be their job, they were awaiting a signal from Harper before lighting torches and setting fire to the cabin.

Pivoting, Starbuck returned to the doorway, the beginning of an idea slowly forming in his mind. Harper, either overconfident or being one man short, was not bothering to post a man in the back yard to watch the rear of the house; and it could be he was simply relying on the pair stationed at the sides to keep it under surveillance. In any event, it offered possibilities—a ray of hope.

Once more inside the cabin, Shawn faced the girl. "Don't think they'll try coming in this way, but stand here where you can watch the yard. You see anything move, shoot."

Dora smiled, took a position at the edge of the door frame. Starbuck recrossed the room to where Ma King stood, peered through the upper half of the glass. The two men in the brush had not moved; Harper was still behind the mound.

"Through talking!" The outlaw's voice was sharp,

impatient. "You're going to make me find out the hard way. All right, up to you. . . . Was only trying to treat you decent."

"Decent—hell!" Ma King shouted. "You don't even know the meaning of the word, Chet Harper!"

"Know what I want—and I aim to get it."

If he was to do anything, he was fast running out of time, Shawn realized. The outlaw would not be held off much longer. Checking his pistol for loads, he looked down at Ma.

"One way maybe I can stop this before it gets going. . . . From the outside."

The older woman wagged her head. "You can't go out there—alone—"

"Spotted the pair Harper's got waiting at the sides of the house," he continued, bypassing her words. "Think his plan is for him and those two over there in the brush to come in shooting. While they're keeping us busy, the others'll slip up from the sides and start the fires. Can block that by getting to them before Harper gives them the signal."

"Risky—"

"Good chance I can make it by keeping low and dodging in and out of the brush clumps."

"But there's two of them. You do manage to get to one, there's still the other'n."

"Reason I'll have to move fast—and I can't see staying in here like rabbits in a trap and letting them roast us alive without putting up a fight."

A brightness came into Ma King's eyes as a tight,

grim smile cracked her lips. "Way I'm looking at it, too. You want me to try sneaking up on one of them?"

Starbuck shook his head. "Better if you'll stay in here, help Aaron. Keep Harper talking long as you can. Need all the time you can buy me."

Aaron said: "What if they open up on us before you get back?"

He hadn't realized King was listening. "Shoot back—don't worry about me, I'll look out for myself. Pretty sure I can stop one of them before he can get a fire going, the other one will depend on luck. . . . I'll face up to the problem when it comes."

Wheeling, Shawn struck for the back entrance in long strides. Ma King's voice followed him.

"Good luck—son."

He grinned, dropped to a crouch, touching Dora with a look as he moved by her.

". . . Waited long enough!" Harper's hard-edged words came from the direction of the mound. "Can see you're just putting me off. You ain't listening to my offers."

"Just that we don't figure we can trust you," Ma answered.

"Trust me—what the hell you want me to do, put it in writing? Give my word—"

Starbuck eased through the doorway, paused on the outside. Pressed flat against the rough logs of the house, he put his attention on the outlaw to his left. The man had dismounted and worked in closer to the cabin. He was poking about, evidently searching for a dry bush or other suitable bit of brush that would serve as a torch. Shawn grunted in satisfaction. He had been right about Harper's plan.

And he was having a bit of luck. From ground level the outlaw was less likely to see him as he probed around than had he still been up in the saddle.

Pistol in hand, Starbuck took a deep breath, flung a last look at the man, back momentarily turned to him, and rushed to gain the first stand of cover. He reached it, hunkered in tight—and then whirled, gun ready, as a sound behind him caught his attention. Anger and surprise rocked him.

It was Dora.

20 ~~~

"What the hell—"

"Wanted to be with you," she answered in a low voice. "Have to talk—"

"Talk!" he echoed in an exasperated whisper. "What the devil's wrong with you? Not the time or the place. You ought to be inside helping Ma and Aaron."

"Nothing I could do—and Ma said it would be all right. . . . No need to watch the back door with you out here."

"Maybe, but you can get hurt—shot."

"Wouldn't matter," Dora said in a worn voice.

Shawn gave her a close, wondering look, felt a stir of pity. Something was disturbing the girl, something deep down and serious—but whatever it was would have to wait. He glanced to the outlaw. The man was standing a few steps in front of his horse, face turned to the mound behind which Chet Harper crouched.

"Stay here," he said. "We'll talk later."

Starbuck again checked the outlaw, reassured himself that the man's attention was centered elsewhere, and, bent low, hurried on to the next large clump of sage. He halted, aware immediately that Dora, like a small, silent shadow, was at his heels. He swung to her, furious.

"Told you to wait!"

The girl's calm features did not alter as her gray eyes met his, held steady. "I'm afraid—by myself."

He swore under his breath, turned back. The outlaw was still waiting for word from Harper. He had kicked loose a fair-size snakeweed, was holding the dry, globe-shaped bush in his left hand. The right was evidently ready with a match.

Starbuck swore again. He had hoped to reach the man, overcome him with a minimum of disturbance so as not to alert the others, and thereby have time in which to double back and take care of the rider on the opposite side of the cabin. His chances for accomplishing this were fading fast; he was now not only hampered by the presence of the girl and would necessarily have to be extra-cautious, but Ma and Aaron had about come to the point where they could stall Harper no further.

"I'll have to move in on him fast," he said, pointing at the outlaw as he tried to make her understand. "Stay here—this time I mean it. Things could go wrong—and he could start shooting."

Dora shook her head. "Only if I have your word you won't leave here without me."

"So that's it!" he said, anger narrowing his eyes. "You think I'm running out on the Kings."

"I—I had to be sure."

"You went to a lot of trouble for nothing. I'll be around until this is all over."

She nodded. "I'll wait," she murmured.

Starbuck turned away, cast a brief look at the outlaw still facing the opposite direction, and moved quietly toward the next bit of cover. Well beyond, at the edge of the yard, he caught a glimpse of Chet Harper once more in the saddle, cutting back to where the remaining outlaws had positioned themselves.

Harper would give the signal for starting the fires when he rejoined them. At that same moment all three would break out, close in on the cabin, firing their guns as they came while the two men on either side of the structure, taking full advantage of its blind walls, would rush in and lay their blazing torches.

That accomplished, their orders undoubtedly then called for them to swing in behind the cabin and cover the back door with a continuing hail of bullets. Thus all those within the house would be effectively pinned down while the flames raged unchecked.

Shawn gained a thick clump of rabbit bush, moved quickly on to a stunted cedar, and halted. The outlaw was no more than a wagon's length away—a tall, blond man. Dismukes, he thought Ma King had called him.

A pistol shot racketed through the late hush. Harper had reached the pair in the brush, was sounding his signal. Dismukes bent forward. A small flame flared in the shelter of his cupped hand. Starbuck, pistol gripped by the barrel, lunged forward, no longer restrained by the need for caution and silence.

The outlaw wheeled at the sound of his approach. His eyes spread with surprise and a yell formed on his lips—but died as Shawn's heavy weapon smashed into the side of his head with a dull thud, dropping him to the ground. Snatching the outlaw's pistol from its holster, he threw it far back into the undergrowth and took up the briskly burning ball of snakeweed. It would be wise to let Harper think all was going as planned.

Holding it to his right in order for the boiling smoke to afford him a screen, he trotted toward the cabin. Reaching the structure, he dropped the flaming brush, being careful to place it a safe distance from the tinder dry wall.

Wheeling at once, he doubled back to where the outlaw lay. Spread out where he had fallen, Dismukes would likely be out of it for several more minutes. When he did recover his senses, he would have neither weapon nor horse and could thus be counted out of the action.

Seizing the reins of the bay the outlaw was riding, Starbuck headed for where he had left Dora. The girl came to her feet as he drew near. Her cheeks were flushed and her eyes bright from excitement.

"Stay low—out of sight," Shawn warned. "Want them to think I'm Dismukes." He continued on without hesitating, striking for the rear of the cabin, as Dora, quickly grasping the idea, crouched low on the opposite side of the horse.

"Got to stop the man on the other—"

His words ended abruptly as smoke rose up from the north side of the cabin, began to stream into the sky. He was too late. The fire had already been started.

Only vaguely aware of the steady thunder of gunshots coming from the front of the structure where the Kings and the outlaws were maintaining a continuing exchange, Shawn released the reins of the horse, which veered away immediately, and started for the opposite corner of the cabin.

Abruptly the rider assigned to that side broke into view. It was Gonzales, the *vaquero*. He was hunched over his saddle, swarthy features set. Their eyes met at the exact same instant. Gonzales' hand swept down for the pistol on his hip. Starbuck snapped a hurried shot. The *vaquero* jolted, buckled, clawed at the outsized horn of his heavy Mexican hull as the horse reared, spun, began to trot off to the left.

Shawn gained the corner of the house, turned. The clumps of brush Gonzales had bunched against the wall were burning fiercely. Small tongues of flames were beginning to appear on the dry logs.

He rushed ahead, hearing the pound of hooves and the hammering of guns still in progress on the hardpack fronting the cabin. Ma and Aaron were apparently matching the outlaws shot for shot. Gagging, choking on the dense, black smoke, he reached the pile of blazing weeds, began to kick it clear of the wall, scatter it. Jerking off his hat, he fell to beating out the dozen or so small fires that were finding purchase on the logs. When the last was dead, he wheeled, ran hard for the brush at the upper edge of the open ground.

He could be seen from the yard, he knew, but he was gambling that Harper and the two men with him would be so occupied they would not notice his passage. Also, layers of smoke from the now-smoldering clumps were drifting across the clearing, affording him a measure of cover.

Starbuck reached the thick growth of sage and rabbit bush, threw himself full length into it. There was little wisdom in going back into the cabin and simply adding his bullets to those of Ma and Aaron. He would do far more good from the outside if he could take a position opposite the structure, set up a crossfire. Once the outlaws realized they were caught in the middle they would quit—but he needed to circle around, get behind the mound of rock from which Harper had done his talking.

Raising himself cautiously, Shawn glanced about, seeking a route that would enable him to reach that point without detection. Motion near the back of the cabin caught his eye. He swore angrily. It was Dora, racing through the haze, to join him.

21 ~~

She paused before him, breast heaving from the effort of running. Starbuck reached out, seized her by the wrist and roughly drew her down beside him.

"Why the hell didn't you stay in the cabin?" he demanded. "You trying to get yourself killed?"

"They couldn't see me," she replied as her breathing evened off. "Anyway, they're too busy with Ma and Aaron—and you promised we could talk."

He stirred irritably. "What've we got to talk about?"

"Me," she answered quietly.

"You've picked a hell of a time to do it," he snapped, and glanced toward the yard.

Harper and his two riders were wheeling in and out, throwing ineffectual shots at the Kings, safe behind the thick walls of their house. The outlaw would be wondering about the fires, cursing his ill luck because both had apparently failed to touch off the structure, impatient for Gonzales and Dismukes to try again.

"What's on your mind?" he asked curtly, turning back to her. He was anxious to let her have her say, get it over with, since there seemed to be no putting it aside. If it had to be, there would come no better moment, as the outlaws were doing no damage.

"I want to go away with you."

"Said that before—and I want to know why. Your place is here."

"Was here," she corrected. "Ollie's the same as dead now. We'll never get married."

So that was it. She had come to the King place intending to be Ollie's wife. Before the marriage could be performed Ollie had gotten into trouble—trouble from which he emerged a hopeless misfit.

"Have you talked to Ma about going?"

Dora nodded. "Just a bit ago—before the outlaws came."

"She agree?"

"Said she wouldn't blame me if I did. Said she could understand that I had nothing to look forward to with Ollie and that I was entitled to have a decent life with a man who would love me and take care of me."

"Must have cost her a lot to tell you that."

"Well, she did. Ask her yourself. . . . She knew I was going to talk to you about it."

Starbuck fell silent, his eyes on the hardpack fronting the cabin. The shooting had ceased and the three outlaws had ridden in behind the mound, probably to discuss the failure of the fires and wonder what had become of their missing partners. In the abrupt hush the mournful plaints of a dove, oddly out of place in those moments, drifted in from the trees to the west.

"Still doesn't seem right, somehow."

"Why not? We were never husband and wife—and if it were me in the same condition, he'd leave me in a minute! Was always going off anyway without giving me a second thought."

Shawn gave that consideration, shrugged. "What do you want me to do?"

"Just what I've said—take me with you. I'll go anywhere, do anything you say. We can be married—"

"No," he cut in, flatly and decisively. "Not in the market for a wife."

"Even if she could give you everything you ever wanted?"

"No, not even that," he answered and then became quiet as the full import of her words registered on him. "Not sure I know what you mean," he added, finally.

Dora faced him coolly. "Means exactly what it sounds like—everything you want; me and what comes with me."

Shawn, again silent, stared at the girl. She had a strength and will he had not suspected, that the quietness of her had hidden.

"Suppose you could give up the search for your brother, could find a fine ranch and settle down, become a cattle grower—get rich and powerful?"

"Can't see that ahead—not for a while—"

"But suppose you could, wouldn't it make you change your mind?"

"No—"

Dora's mouth drew into a petulant line. "Why not? What's wrong with me? Don't you think I'm pretty enough?"

"Not that. Just that I'll get what I want the way a man usually does—by working for it."

"That would take years. Why waste them when you could have it all now?"

Starbuck shrugged impatiently. "You're talking bosh! Even if I was interested, how could you—"

He paused, realization like a shaft of light freed by his own question, flooding across his mind. He grasped her by the arms, drew her close, stared at her intently.

"Just now came to me—how could you do all that for a man?"

"I can—and would for the right one."

He shook her roughly. "How?"

"I—I know where the gold's hid!"

Starbuck's jaw tightened as anger rushed through him. "You know—and you let Harper and his gang make war on the Kings!"

"I wasn't afraid for them after you came—and besides, why should I give it to Chet Harper just so's he'll leave them alone? He and his bunch will go away as soon as they decided Aaron doesn't know where the money is, anyway."

"But in the meanwhile there'll be some killings over it, maybe even Ma—"

"Not likely."

"No? You think they're playing games out there, using cotton balls for bullets? I've already shot one man."

"A Mexican—an outlaw."

"A man just the same, and before this is over with, there'll be more go down. Stand a damned good chance of stopping lead myself—while all the time you're sitting back with the key, with the thing that can stop it!"

"It's my gold. Ollie sent me a map in a letter he wrote me before they took him off to the pen. Told me to hang onto it until he came back. It's no good to him. The whole fifty thousand dollars won't help him one whit—so it's mine."

Shawn shrugged wearily at such reasoning. "Wasn't Ollie's in the first place. . . . Ma know about this, too?"

"No, of course not. But if she did she'd tell me to take it and run—do what I'm intending to do. Ma's a woman. She know's what a woman's up against in this country, believes in grabbing what she can and hanging onto it."

"Doubt that, Dora. She wasn't talking about the gold if she said it."

"I know Ma King pretty well—and I think she'd feel the same way about it. She lost her man, had to slave to keep herself and her boys alive. Still doing it, in fact—but she'd be practical about the money."

Shawn looked out across the yard to the mound of brush and rocks. The outlaws had not moved. "You've been around Ma a lot longer than I have and maybe you know her better. Could be I've misjudged her—but that's neither here nor there. The gold's not yours. It has to go back to the people it belongs to—Well-Fargo."

"No—never!" Dora said in a quick, firm way. "I'm offering it—a share of it—to you if you'll take me to where it's buried and help me get it. After that, if you don't want me, all I'm asking is that you see me to some town where I can be on my own. . . . If you're not willing, I'll make other plans."

"Go get it by yourself?"

Dora's shoulders stirred. "I'm not that simple-minded. I'll need help—a man's help."

"Which will mean taking in a partner."

"That's what he'll be."

Starbuck smiled at her. "Not much choice around here. Got anybody in mind?"

"Chet Harper."

He stared at her incredulously. "You think you can deal with him? He'll agree, sure, but once the gold is in his hands you'll never see him or it again! Truth is, you'll be lucky to get out of it alive."

Dora looked down, bit at her lower lip. "That's why I wanted you, Starbuck. I know I can trust you."

He shook his head. "Count me out. I want no part of it, and if I've got anything to say, the map will go to Wells-Fargo—"

"But you don't," she cut in, abruptly cool. "It's mine and I'm going to keep it, and if you turn me down, I'll think of something else—either chance Harper or maybe I'll just go it alone, let it stay where it is until someday I can find the right man who'll see things my way."

"He probably won't be hard to meet—"

"And don't think you can leave here and go running to some lawman about it," she broke in. "I'll be gone by the time he could get back."

131

"If any of us leave here," Starbuck murmured, again shifting his eyes to the outlaws. He drew up sharply. They were filing out from behind the mound. Evidently they had concluded something had happened to Gonzales and Dismukes, were now changing their plans.

"If so, it won't matter. The gold wouldn't do me any good. . . . Nobody else will get it either."

"Odds are mighty good that's the way it'll work out," Shawn said, eyes still on Chet Harper and the two men with him.

Dora gripped his arm suddenly, looked up into his grim face. "Starbuck, think about it again. Don't say no! There's so much we can have, so much good life ahead of us if you'll take it. With all that money we can have everything we ever wanted—go to all the places we've dreamed of visiting."

He did not respond, simply continued to watch the outlaws.

"It can be on your terms. If you don't want me for a wife, then take me as a woman—I'll be happy and satisfied."

"There'd be no happiness," he said. "We'd always be thinking about that gold—where it came from, how we got it. You can't build anything good on that kind of a foundation."

"But we could—I know we could! And we can leave here right now while everything is quiet. Your horse is in the barn. I can use the one Dismukes was riding."

"And just forget Ma and Aaron, and all this trouble?"

"They'll be all right. Harper won't hurt them when he finds out Aaron can't tell them what he wants to know."

"Can believe that. It's the in-between that worries me—the time when all the shooting will go on before he decides Aaron doesn't know."

"Then why can't we have Ma tell him—after we've gone—that we've got the map—"

Starbuck wasn't listening. The outlaws were swinging in toward the cabin. A rifle blasted the hush, sending up a chain of rolling echoes. The man to the left of Harper flinched, then laughed.

"I'm getting in behind them," Shawn said, his features tightening. "Aim to stop this before it gets any worse. . . . Best you stay here."

Dora shook her head stubbornly, smiled. "I'm coming with you. I still think you'll change your mind."

22 ~~~

Starbuck cut back through the brush, circled toward the mound. Harper and the men siding him had now halted a distance below it, eyes on the figure of Dismukes, walking unsteadily across the flat. The outlaw, hat in one hand, was holding a wadded bandana to his head with the other. There was no sign of the *vaquero*.

Shawn gained a hedge of waist-high sage to the north of the rocks, halted. Dora, never more than a step behind him, hunched close by.

"Maybe they'll give up now," she said tautly.

"Doubt it," he replied. "Fifty thousand is a lot of money—and Harper's not the quitting kind."

"It can be yours—ours."

He turned, looked down at her. "Don't start that again!"

"But why? Don't you want a lot of money?"

"Nothing wrong with that. Would be a fine thing having all you needed and being able to do what you've always wanted to do, but there'd be no peace inside me. I'd always remember that I had no right to it."

"Just having it makes it your right. Out here you have to look out for yourself, take what you can and hold onto it. There's such a thing as not being practical—of being too honest."

A half smile pulled at Starbuck's lips. "I don't think so. You can't be too honest or just a little honest. Either you are or you aren't."

Harper and his men had now pulled off to the south edge of the yard and intercepted Dismukes. They were grouped before him in a half circle while he talked, apparently relating what had occurred.

"Time we got into those rocks," Shawn said. "Things are going to bust wide open here in a few minutes."

Turning, he dropped farther back into the feathery, blue-gray undergrowth, and, keeping low, trotted the remaining distance to the tumbled mass of brush and rocks.

Climbing halfway to its summit, Shawn drew in

behind a large boulder and swung his attention to the far side of the cleared flat. Dismukes was walking slowly on toward the dense brush to the east; Harper and the others were separating, one man curving in to the south wall of the cabin, another angling for the opposite side—following a course that would bring him close to the mound—while the outlaw leader himself moved cautiously on a direct line for the front of the squat, log structure.

"You come too close, Chet Harper, and I'll shoot you off'n that saddle!"

Ma King's voice crackled through the afternoon sunlight.

"Ain't never killed a man yet but that ain't saying I can't!"

Harper pulled up. "You ain't done much good so far—and I expect you're 'most out of bullets. . . . Better trot Aaron out so's I can talk to him."

"Tired of telling you—he ain't got nothing to say. Now, take your bunch and get out of here—you seen what happened to Dismukes, and the Mex ain't around no more, either."

"Makes no difference."

"Well, it ought to. Starbuck's still out there somewheres and what happened to them's going to happen to the rest of you unless you move on."

"I ain't worrying about Starbuck, whoever he is."

"You better be—only three of you left."

Shawn watched the rider slanting toward the mound with narrowed eyes, striving to guess the path he would take—one crossing in front of them, or one behind.

"He's the one they call Georgia," Dora said in a low voice. "Other one heading for the back is Bill Drake."

"It's Georgia we need to think about," Shawn replied. "Likely be some shooting when he gets here. Want you to ease down behind those rocks. Be safe there."

Dora gave him a quick, hopeful look. "That mean you've changed your mind about me and—"

"Just don't want you hurt," he said, shaking his head.

Her shoulders sagged, and, turning about, she crawled into the hollow a yard or two below where he crouched.

Georgia, eyes on Harper, bore in steadily. It made no particular difference to Starbuck which route the outlaw chose; to him it was simply a matter of being prepared to act. He hoped he could take the man without gunplay; shooting would immediately draw Harper and Bill Drake, whereas eliminating the man quickly and quietly, as he had Dismukes, would enable him to remain unhampered, free to move about and in good position to further lower the odds.

The outlaw drew near, veering slightly left. He had elected to cross in front. Starbuck, hunched low, fell back, hurriedly circled the formation, and gained its lower end. Gun still holstered, he waited behind a shoulder of granite, poised to spring. Georgia moved up, came abreast—passed by.

Starbuck threw himself from the corner of the rock.

His fingers caught at the man's arms, locked around fabric of his shirt. Throwing his weight to the side, he dragged the outlaw from the saddle.

They hit the ground solidly as Georgia's horse shied away. Cursing savagely, the outlaw struggled to get at the pistol pinned beneath him. Shawn pulled back, swung a blow at the man's jaw—missed.

"Hey—over here!"

The yell broke from Georgia's mouth before Starbuck could prevent it. He lashed out again at the outlaw's head, but the man jerked aside again, rolled to his knees. On beyond him, Starbuck could see Harper coming up fast, ignoring the shots directed at him by Ma and Aaron as they sought to help.

Georgia's hand flashed down, came up. The slanting rays of the sun glinted off the pistol clutched in his fingers. Shawn lunged to his left, fired, all in one single motion. Georgia rocked back on his haunches, hung briefly, and toppled.

Starbuck spun to face Chet Harper. The outlaw leader, now in range, snapped a bullet at him. Shawn flinched as it grazed his arm, struck the granite behind him, and noisily sang off into space. Dropping to his knees, he triggered a shot at the onrushing man, swore as the lead went wide.

He threw himself full length, taking what cover he could find. A second bullet ripped through the cloth of his corded pants, seared a stinging groove across his thigh. Cursing, he steadied the weapon in his hand, pressed off a shot.

Chet Harper yelled, buckled. His horse, suddenly without a firm hand on the leathers, swerved, began to lope toward Georgia's mount, which was standing head up, ears pricked forward, in the brush a hundred yards or so farther on. The outlaw, one arm dangling loosely at his side, gripped the horn of his saddle as, bouncing like a rag doll, he fought to stay upright.

Shawn, feeling the warm, stickiness of blood trickling down his leg, drew back into the rocks. Thumbing cartridges from his belt, he reloaded quickly. There was still Bill Drake to account for. Pistol cylinder full, he circled to where Dora waited, climbed on to the forward edge of the mound as she eyed him anxiously.

"You've been shot!"

"Only a scratch," he said, dismissing her alarm.

Turning toward the cabin, he came to sudden attention. Drake was moving toward him, arms raised, palms flat to show he had holstered his weapon. Shawn rose to full height, and, gun leveled at the man, waited for him to get near. . . . Evidently Drake wanted no more of it, was quitting.

"Don't shoot!" the man called as he approached the mound. "I'm leaving."

Starbuck nodded coldly. "Pull your gun—let it drop."

Drake, face shining with sweat, reached for the pistol on his hip. Lifting it carefully with the tips of his fingers, he allowed it to fall.

"Now move on," Shawn snapped. "Get your friends and ride out—and keep remembering I'll be standing here watching everything you do."

Bill Drake bobbed his head. "Was ready to go a hour back, only Harper wouldn't listen. Way I seen it the Kings was telling the truth."

"They are. They don't know where that gold's buried."

The outlaw mumbled something, jerked a thumb in the direction of Harper, still in the saddle. His horse had halted beside Georgia's.

"Aim to catch up the bay and take him to Dave so's he'll have something to ride. That all right with you?"

"All right—"

Drake clucked at his mount and moved on. He came alongside the sprawled figure of Georgia, paused to look down. After a moment he shook his head.

"Old Georgia was wanting to pull out, too, same as me, but we just couldn't make Chet listen. . . . You see he gets a burying?"

Starbuck nodded, watched the outlaw ride on, reach Harper and the stray horse. Drake, leaning over, gathered up the reins of the two animals, and, with the outlaw leader clinging tight to the horn, led them off toward the brush where Dismukes had vanished.

Shawn heard the light crunch of gravel as Dora climbed up beside him.

"I—I guess it's all over."

Gaze still on the receding outlaws, Shawn holstered his weapon. "Finished," he said quietly.

She moved around to where she could face him directly. "Do you still feel the same—about me and the gold, I mean?"

"Nothing's changed."

A small sound escaped her throat as she looked away. Then, "Are you going to tell Ma about me having the map and knowing all the time where the gold's buried?"

He was silent for a time, finally shrugged. "No, that's up to you."

"Then I can keep it?"

"Have to decide that for yourself. You're the one who'll have to live with whatever it is you do. . . . Come on, best we get back to the house. Could be Ma or Aaron got hurt."

He took the girl's hand to steady her, and together they climbed down from the crest of the mound and headed across the flat to the cabin.

23 ~~~

Starbuck slowed his step, an uneasiness moving through him. He had expected the cabin door to swing open when they drew near, see Ma and Aaron standing there, hear them sing out. The offhand statement he'd made only a few minutes earlier to Dora concerning the possibility of the Kings being injured abruptly assumed solid reality.

"Something's wrong—"

He broke into a run as he muttered the words, and, ignoring pain in his leg, hurried on. The girl kept pace with him. They reached the structure. Extending his hand, he grasped the latch, flung the panel back, and rushed into the dim interior.

"Ma?"

In that same fraction of time Starbuck pulled up short. Ma King was standing against the wall. Next to her, arms raised, was Aaron, and, facing him as he entered, a pistol in each hand was, Luke Hillister.

A gasp of fear broke from Dora's lips at sight of the towering, black-bearded man. Impulsively she caught at Shawn's wrist.

"Who—"

"The bounty hunter—the one I came to warn you about."

Hillister, eyes like glowing coals in the basket of his dark face, motioned to Starbuck, directed him to turn about.

"Sure wasn't looking to find you here, too, bucko," he rumbled in his deep voice as he stepped up, lifted Shawn's weapon from its leather. "Reckon I got me a real passel of prizes this time. . . . You get out of the way now, missy. Just stand there by your ma."

Starbuck pivoted slowly, seeing Dora cross the room quickly to the side of Ma King.

"You've got no call coming here, Hillister," he said angrily. He was blaming himself for his own carelessness. If he'd stopped to think instead of pounding up to the door like some wet-eared kid—

"No? Ain't these folks the Kings?"

"They are, but they're not wanted."

Luke Hillister wagged his massive head. "I know better'n that. Was them that done that robbing up Colorado way."

"Not saying it wasn't, but they went to the pen for it."

"Out now, ain't they?"

"They were pardoned—served all the time the law figured was needful."

"Law was wrong," the bounty hunter declared stubbornly. "They still got to pay. Wasn't right they was turned loose, and I aim to—"

"Listen to me, Hillister! The law's through with them—doesn't want them back—same as it doesn't want me."

"Ain't sure of that, either."

"You ought to be!" Starbuck snapped. "You saw the Cimarron sheriff look me up. You heard him say I wasn't an outlaw."

"Hell, old Bart Trueman don't know nothing. I'm betting the next sheriff I go to'll be real glad to see you, same as he will the Kings. . . . Where's the other boy?"

Starbuck sighed in disgust. He'd known it was useless to try and reason with Luke Hillister, but he had to make the effort. Turning away, he glanced about the cabin seeking an idea, a means for overcoming the bounty hunter. The rifles and shotgun were propped against the wall near the bench where the spare ammunition had been piled. His own weapon was tucked under the waistband of Hillister's pants.

Wait . . . Hold off, he cautioned himself. *You'll only get yourself and some of the others hurt if you try anything while he's holding those two cocked pistols on you.*

Ma King, elbows bent, hands folded under her apron in womanly fashion, touched him with her eyes, then let them move on to Hillister.

"You're wasting your time, mister," she said. "The law ain't after my boys."

"I am," he answered flatly. "Where's the other'n?"

"Reckon you'll just have to find him yourself. I sure ain't telling you."

"Suits me," the bearded man said, his broad, thick shoulders stirring.

Hillister backed to where Starbuck stood against the door. Motioning again at him with one of his weapons, he said: "Get over there with them others."

Shawn crossed slowly, nerves razor sharp, muscles taut; if he could somehow throw himself to the side, snatch up one of the rifles—get to the hidden knife in his boot.

"Don't you go trying something cute," Hillister warned softly, reading his mind. "I only got to squeeze a trigger and you ain't got no head!"

The bounty hunter laughed at the sound of his own words, cackling in an odd, broken way. In the breathless quiet that filled the cabin, Starbuck glanced at the Kings and Dora. Aaron, arms still held aloft, and the girl were rigid, fear drawing their features into harsh, flat planes. Ma's sun-browned, lined face was expressionless, but her eyes were sharp, calculating.

Reaching the wall, Shawn stepped in beside Aaron. Luke Hillister holstered the weapon he was holding in his left hand, opened the door. Then, taking a step to the side, he gathered up the two rifles and the shotgun in his hamlike fist, carried them to the opening, and flung them into the yard. That done, he kneed the panel closed.

"That's so's you won't get no ideas," he said, grinning at Starbuck. His dark, heavy-lidded eyes swept the cabin, halted on Ma King. "Ain't you got no rope in here, missus?"

"Out in the barn," she replied cooly. "You want it—go get it."

The bounty hunter favored her with a hard grin. "Trying to trick me, eh? Well, you ain't about to. I know what I'm doing."

Shawn watched the bounty hunter edge toward the bunks built against the wall. He had slipped in through the back while Ma and Aaron were at the windows, busy fighting off Chet Harper and the others, he guessed. Likely it had been all the shooting that had attracted him to the cabin and divulged the location of the family.

"This'll do good as rope," Hillister said, jerking a blanket from the top bunk. Bunching it in his hand, he tossed it to Starbuck. "Get busy tearing that into strips so's—"

Luke paused, his gaze reaching through the opening that led into Ma's bedroom. He grinned widely, exposing his strong teeth.

"Well, what d'you know! Here's that other boy—a-hiding under the covers like a scared little rabbit!"

"You leave him be!" Ma shouted.

Careful to keep his weapon leveled at them all, still grinning, the bounty hunter leaned to the side, grasped Ollie by the ankle and dragged him off the bed.

"Get up little rabbit—and get in here!"

Ollie struggled to a sitting position and stared blankly around the room. Hillister swung his leg, kicked him brutally in the ribs. The younger King recoiled in pain, cried out.

Ma surged forward, eyes blazing. "Cut that out! Can't you see he don't know what you're saying? He ain't right in the head!"

She halted as Hillister threatened her with the gun. The bounty hunter reached down, caught Ollie by the arm and jerked him upright, shoved him stumbling toward the others. Dora caught him by the hand, pulled him in to her side.

"You got that blanket tore up?" Luke shouted, turning his attention on Starbuck. He was suddenly angry, his eyes raging, his mouth trembling as he spoke. "Get to doing it so's we can get out of here. I'm tired of fooling around!"

"Be dark pretty quick," Shawn said in a voice pitched to calm the violence boiling through the bearded man. "Why don't you figure to stay here 'til morning, have a bite to eat—rest?"

"Hell with waiting!" Hillister screamed. "I'm taking the three of you right now soon's—"

"You ain't taking nobody—no place!" Ma King cried.

Her hands came out from beneath the apron. In one

145

she held the old Navy Colt, overlooked by Hillister when he took a rifle from her. She triggered the heavy weapon fast but the cloth of the apron had snagged on the hammer. The bullet thudded into the wall behind the bounty hunter, missed narrowly.

Luke Hillister fired in the same moment. Ma staggered back as the load smashed into her, drove her to the floor while the cabin rocked with the blasts of the two guns overridden only by Dora's screams.

Starbuck leaped forward through the layers of smoke, hurling the blanket into the bounty hunter's face as he did. Hillister brushed it aside, endeavored to avoid Shawn's rush. He failed and the two men came together in a solid collision. The impetus carried Luke backwards, slammed him against the wall. Starbuck rebounded, struck out with his balled fist.

The blow only grazed Hillister's jaw, evoked a stream of curses. The bounty hunter swung his pistol at Shawn's head, caught him high on the neck. Starbuck went to his knees, instinctively rocked to one side. A knee smashed into his shoulder, knocked him out of the way. He looked up. Aaron King, Ma's pistol in his fist, mouth blared wide in a cry of anguish and hate, eyes blazing, stood over him.

The Colt began to blast. Once . . . Twice—several times until it was empty. Luke Hillister, as if pinned against the wall, hung there, half bent, his huge body jolting each time a bullet struck him. When the deafening thunder had finally ceased, he remained motionless, bearded face tipped down, and then abruptly his massive body toppled to the floor like some giant tree felled by a mighty wind.

Shawn drew himself upright, stepped to the door, and opened it to thin out the drifting clouds of acrid, choking smoke. Turning, he crossed to where Dora and Aaron knelt beside Ma King. Beyond them Ollie had found a chair, was sitting down.

The girl, holding the older woman's head in her lap, looked up at Starbuck as he hunched beside her.

"Ma's dead," she murmured, voice breaking. "She—she said she loved me—and called me daughter."

Shawn looked away. After a time he slipped his arms under the slight body and stood up. As he turned for the bedroom Aaron stepped in close, his arms extended.

"Let me have her," he said tightly, "She's my ma."

Starbuck released his burden, fell back, watched King carry the still figure into the makeshift room and lay it on the bed. A bitter thought pushed into his mind: Aaron had found himself at last—but it was too late. Ma would never know.

24 ~~~

Starbuck folded his arms across his chest, and, leaning against the thick-trunked old cottonwood growing in solitary majesty on the slope rising before him, lowered his head. Farther up the gentle grade a square of whitewashed stones outlined the King family cemetery. The lone grave within its boundaries now had a companion.

The night before he and Aaron had nailed together a pine coffin, and then, with the morning sun slanting down from a clear sky, they had laid Ma, clad in her one Sunday dress—a crisp, black satin trimmed in yellowing lace—beside the man who had meant so much to her.

Well before that they had buried Hillister and Georgia in a place some distance from the area. Shawn had scratched their names, such as he knew them, into headboards and driven them deep into the soil to mark the location. Aaron had felt that neither was entitled to the smallest commemoration, but Starbuck performed the chore, anyway; outlaws undeniably, they were still men and, despite their imperfections, their passing should be noted.

Aaron had taken the death of Ma hard, but it also had changed him, turned him from a passive, ineffectual man to one of firmness and decisiveness. It was as if the loss had jarred him from the apathy of indifference, causing him to finally assume the role he had avoided.

Starbuck raised his eyes as the last words of the familiar prayer being quoted by Dora reached him. Motionless, he watched King, one hand gripping the arm of his brother, turn from the grave and start down the slope. The girl stepped in beside Ollie, took his other arm, and together the three approached Shawn.

"Reckon we've done the best we could for her," Aaron said quietly, halting. He released Ollie, allowed Dora to continue on to the house with him. "Hard to find the words so's I can say how grateful we are."

"No need."

"There's plenty need. Most men would never bothered to do what you done—especially did they know who it was they were helping. . . . Us Kings have always been plenty short on friends."

"Maybe you never gave folks a chance. Man has to go halfway himself. Can't expect others to do it all."

"Could be you're right—and things are going to change some. Aim to see to that." Aaron paused, stared off across the rolling hillscape. He seemed unwilling to look at Starbuck as he voiced his question.

"You taking Dora with you?"

Shawn frowned. "You know about that?"

"Ma told me. Said she was set on being your woman."

"Her idea—not mine. Happens there's no place in my life for a woman—not yet, anyway. Would be only a matter of helping her get to the next town."

"Then you ain't wanting her?" There was a faint hoarseness to Aaron King's voice.

"Like I said—just helping."

"She know that?"

"Made it plain as I could." Starbuck considered the man intently. "Dora means a lot to you—can see that."

Aaron shrugged despairingly. "Just wish you wouldn't take her—"

"Neither here nor there with me. Leaving it up to Dora."

"She never had nothing here 'cepting hard work, so I can't blame her for wanting to go. . . . I'd change all that, was she to stay—make it all up to her."

"Might try telling her that."

In his mind Shawn doubted it would mean anything to the girl. She felt cheated by life, and now with the promise of the gold Ollie had hidden away at her disposal, she had visions of enjoying all the good things she believed had passed her by.

"Maybe she wouldn't listen. Always wanted to talk to her, say things, but she was Ollie's girl—and I didn't think it'd be decent—even after we come back from the pen."

"It would've helped if you had. Nobody ever took the time to tell her how they felt, that she was loved and wanted. . . . Something you can fix right now," he added, ducking his head at the girl moving slowly along the path as she returned from the cabin. "I'll be saddling my horse. Time I was heading out for Santa Fe."

He cut away from the slope, slanting through the dappled shade toward the barn where the sorrel was stabled.

"Starbuck—"

At Dora's call Shawn halted. He nodded at King still standing under the cottonwood, head bowed, hands locked behind his back.

"Aaron wants to talk to you."

She paused, studied the lonely figure briefly as interest brightened her eyes, and then turned back to Starbuck.

"Are you leaving now?"

"Soon as I get my horse ready. If you're riding with me, get your things together."

She crossed to him, her features calm, set. "You'd take me with you?"

"If that's what you want."

Dora smiled, seemingly pleased with the knowledge. "Thank you," she murmured, "but I've changed my mind. I'm going to stay."

Wordless, he stared at her.

"I'm not sure why. Something Ma said, I guess, or maybe it was you—or him," she added, glancing again at Aaron. "He's changed."

"He'll do fine now."

"I know—and I'll help him," she said, and extended her hand. "Goodbye—"

He took her fingers into his, felt the edges of a folded piece of paper in his palm, frowned.

"It's the map," Dora said. "I'm asking you to give it to the law. . . . I don't want the gold."

Starbuck slipped the creased sheet into a pocket, smiled. "It's the right thing to do. It could never buy you what you really want."

Bending forward he kissed her lightly on the forehead. "So long," he said, and continued toward the barn and the waiting sorrel.

Center Point Publishing
600 Brooks Road ● PO Box 1
Thorndike ME 04986-0001 USA

(207) 568-3717

US & Canada:
1 800 929-9108
www.centerpointlargeprint.com